One Shot Too Many

Other Books by
Maggie Bishop

Appalachian Adventure Romances
Appalachian Paradise
Emeralds in the Snow

Appalachian Adventure Mysteries
Murder at Blue Falls
Perfect for Framing

One Shot Too Many

Appalachian Adventure Mystery by

Maggie Bishop

INGALLS PUBLISHING GROUP, INC

INGALLS PUBLISHING GROUP, INC
PO Box 2500
Banner Elk, NC 28604
www.ingallspublishinggroup.com

copyright © 2011 Maggie Bishop
Text design by Judith Geary
Cover design by: Luci Mott
Cover photograph by Maggie Bishop

This book is a work of fiction. All characters, places and incidents are either the product of the author's imagination or are used fictiously, and any resemblance to persons living or dead, business establishments, events or locales in entirely coincidental.

Without limiting the rights reserved under copyright above, no part of this publication may be reproduced, stored or entered into a retrieval system or transmitted, in any form or by any means (electronic, mechanical, photocopying, recording or otherwise), without the prior written permission of both the copyright owner and the above publisher of this book. Exception to this prohibition is permitted for limited quotations included within a published review of the book.

The scanning, uploading and distribution of this book via the internet or via any other means without the permission of the publisher is illegal and punishable by law. Please purchase only authorized editions and do not participate in or encourage piracy of copyrighted materials. Your support of author's rights is appreciated.

Library of Congress Cataloging-in-Publication Data

Bishop, Maggie, 1949-
One shot too many / by Maggie Bishop.
p. cm. -- (Appalachian adventure mystery ; v. 3)
ISBN 978-1-932158-95-3 (trade pbk. : alk. paper)
1. Murder--Investigation--Fiction. 2. Appalachian Region, Southern--Fiction. 3. North Carolina--Fiction. I. Title.
PS3602.I76O57 2011
813'.6--dc22
                   2010053488

Dedicated to:
Lyle D. Bishop, II
1918-2010
loving husband to Pearl Louise Munn Bishop,
father to the author, career US Air Force,
ski patrol, fire fighter and first responder.

Acknowledgments

Husband Bob Gillman for love and patience
Parents Pearle & Lyle Bishop for love
and my first computer
Judith Geary, IPG editor &
author of the Getorix series
Barbara & Bob Ingalls, publishers,
for believing in my stories
Dee Dee Rominger, Captain of Investigations,
Watauga County Sheriff's department
Jane Wilson, author, for use of her recipes from
Mountain Born and Fed
Ree Strawser for photography information
Rex and Aileen Frederick, of the
Clear Creek Guest Ranch in Burnsville, NC
for their hospitality
Crossed Sabres Ranch, Cody, Wyoming,
Powderhorn Guest Ranch, Powderhorn, Colorado,
Ridin'-Hy Ranch Resort, Warrensburg, NY

Blue Falls Ranch Schedule of Events

Sunday: Guests arrive, settle in room and relax
4 pm - Wine and cheese and ranch tour
Monday:
9 am - Riding Orientation and trail ride to introduce guests to horses
2 pm - Trail ride along Elk Creek to East Ridge
Non Riders, meet at 1:00 to visit downtown Boone and ASU's Turchin Art Center
Evening - Sunset hike, game room
Tuesday:
9 am - Trail ride to Tail Feather Cove
2 pm - Trail ride to Racoon Run
Non riders, meet at front desk at 1 pm to visit Banner Elk Winery
Evening - movie and popcorn
Wednesday:
9 am - Trail ride past Racoon Run to ridge
2 pm - Trail ride to Rhymer Hill
Non riders, meet at front desk at 1 pm for Blue Ridge Parkway bike ride
Evening - Steak cookout with mountain music with our own **Wrangler Bo**

Thursday:
9 am - Trail ride to Secret Location
2 pm - Trail ride to Deer Springs
Non riders, meet at front desk 9:30 am for Grandfather Mtn. Biosphere visit
Evening - Square Dancing in dining room, costumes available

Friday:
9:30 am - All day trail ride and picnic to Whisky Ridge
Non riders, visit Moses Cone Mansion & Parkway Craft Center on Blue Ridge Parkway
Evening - Local storyteller **Jane Wilson** to tell *Jane Tales* by the camp fire

Saturday:
8 am - All day trail ride with breakfast cookout to Blue Falls waterfall
Non riders, visit historic downtown Boone and Artwalk Gallery
Evening - Gymkhana Competition
Sunday Morning: check out and hugs goodby

Remember to pick up your photo CD

Major Characters

Jemma Chase - Trail ride leader, photographer, carpenter and CSI wannabe
Detective Tucker - Watauga County Sheriff's Department detective
Detective Graves - Detective Tucker's partner
Scott Barker - Newspaper photographer
Roger Davis - Judge
Tammy Portsmith - Nurse
Aaron Wyman - Dental Hygienist
Harold Bench - Retired Army
Summer Miller - Sports Trainer
Leslie Fine - Grandmother and gardener
Wanda - Tucker's old girlfriend
Alma Chase - Blue Falls Ranch Chef, Jemma's aunt.
Bo-Head Wrangler
Miguel-Wrangler
Juanita - Cook

Chapter 1: Monday Afternoon, early June

Detective Tucker had always heard that if you were going to sin, figure out who to tell or join the Catholic Church, even here in the Bible belt. Past sins denied were to the psyche like a web woven in the night poised to smack you in the face on that narrow trail.

Tucker headed back to his partner in the idling county vehicle. Tiny warning hairs on the back of his neck quivered, signaling danger. Thunder roiled loud and long, echoing a gut feel that something criminal was about to happen.

He looked back over his shoulder. Lightning crackled overhead then focused full force on a tree not a hundred feet behind him. Tucker stuck his fingers in his ears when the resulting boom reverberated in the nearby Blue Ridge Parkway underpass.

Acrid smoke from a newly blacked streak down the length of a large poplar snag filled his nose but no fire broke out. He bolted down the highway berm as the lightning-struck dead tree, not a hundred feet away, crashed down as if directed straight at him. Close call, he thought, as the jolt of adrenalin passed through him.

At least the rain held off, a relief after twenty-eight straight days of downpours in these North Carolina mountains. The official three-year drought was over. The unusually hot eighty degrees made the place feel dank and damp as a rain forest. Graves, his partner, answered a call and motioned Tucker to the county SUV.

Tucker punched the voice mail button on his cell phone while jogging the last few yards to the county vehicle.

"I swear I'm not involved," Jemma's message said. Tucker buckled his seat belt as Detective Graves drove the patrol car. He put Jemma's message on speaker phone. "Someone keeled over in the game room at Blue Falls Ranch. I called 911 to get the ambulance. Come quickly. A nurse attending our photography club meeting is doing compressions. I'll get the defibrillator. Something's not right."

Her voice relayed an undercurrent of excitement Tucker had learned meant her CSI wannabe tendencies had kicked in. "He's my age, in his 30s, healthy, friendly. We think it's poison. Gotta go. I've moved everyone but the nurse out into the dining room."

Jemma Chase had called his cell phone and left that message while he'd nearly been zapped by lightning. He concentrated to conrol the grin that his partner said came on his face every time he heard her voice.

Graves confirmed that dispatch directed them to proceed to the scene. The investigation of vandals painting the underpass could wait. Wish they'd grow up and find a real life, he thought as Detective Graves drove the steep winding Elk Creek Road down the mountain to Triplett Valley. The road dropped a thousand feet in three miles to the lowest point in Watauga County, around seventeen hundred feet in elevation. Another murder, suspicious death, according to Jemma. She'd had enough experience in that area to know. Tucker gripped the overhead handle to stabilize himself while Graves took the last three curves a little too fast. Luckily, no other vehicles approached on the narrow sixteen foot asphalt road.

Still no rain but lots of thunder and lightning as they drove on to the Blue Falls Ranch property, under the rustic sign supported by hand-hewn posts imbedded on either side of the gravel road. A couple of horses dashed madly toward the barn, tails high, within the white rail fence in the pasture on the right. A pond with benches and trees glistened between the corral and circular drive. The ranch road followed a fast flowing creek for the first quarter mile then veered to the right. A wide circular drive led to the two-storied log lodge, reminiscent of the national park lodges out west. Five rustic duplex cabins sat back from the winding creek. Tucker glimpsed Jemma's own cabin on the far side of the creek, off by itself.

Tucker and Graves split up and quickly photographed all the vehicles parked outside the lodge, including the jumble of cars, with portable red lights attached to the roofs, belonging to first responders. Never knew which evidence was key in a suspected homicide. If it proved to be a natural death, all that was lost was some time and effort.

Tucker photographed the dozen steps up to the main lodge then ran up them and into the lodge, heading to the game room. He nodded to Jemma's parents, the ranch owners, standing outside the dining room. Tucker's own heart thumped when the first responders applied the defibrillator shock to the man on the floor. Scott was someone he'd known for a long time. His upper body jumped inches off the floor with the jolt. He could have sworn he saw Scott's haint hover above his body then float away. Too much coffee. Too many ghost stories told around the wood stove when he was a kid.

Tucker looked around the game room while the whine of the defib recharge filled the silence.

Photographs and papers littered three tables near the body. At Tucker's glance, the first responder shook his head, confirming what Tucker already knew. The second jolt hadn't restarted the heart. Too young to die. Scott Barker had gone to school with Tucker's younger cousin. He'd have to call Scott's parents once he was officially pronounced by the Medical Examiner at the hospital. The ex-wife should be told, too, he thought as he photographed the body. Years of experience had made the task familiar but not easier. He could hand off that job to someone else but he'd been friends with Scott. The photos might reveal information about who and why someone wanted him dead.

Then he joined Graves in the dining room. Smart of Jemma to clear the scene of unnecessary people. Jemma stood apart from the two quiet groups clustered over by the coffee pot. A nod in her direction was all he allowed himself. Couldn't think about their last night together, had to focus. He'd sort out the "conflict of interest" argument with the Chief later. Jemma did have a knack for being around the only unnatural deaths in Watauga County lately. At least this time she'd called 911 immediately and then called him. She'd better leave the investigating to him. He was in charge. Tucker nodded to his partner, Graves. "You take the six in the group to the left. And Jemma. I'll take the other group."

A rotund man with a military stance offered his hand. "How Is Scott? I'm Harold, president of this photography club."

"We would like to talk to each of you separately." Tucker shook the hand then diverted everyone's attention. "Please have a seat and refrain from talking."

"Why? What's happened? Is he dead?" Harold persisted.

"He's not responding. This is routine. We'll get to you as soon as we can. You, too." He nodded at Jemma. The ambulance arrived; the paramedics consulted with the first responders then loaded the body onto the stretcher and carried it down the steps to the ambulance.

Tucker pulled aside the lead paramedic. "Be sure to have the M. E. take both cut and pulled hair samples and nail clippings. He'll have to send his poison testing results to Chapel Hill." Tucker frowned. "I'll leave the choice of which poisons to request since I'm not sure." The paramedic wrote in a notebook and left.

Graves wrote down the names of those who responded to the call. The first responders left at the same time since they had not been on site at the time of the possible crime. Jemma's parents returned to work for the same reason.

Tucker called to update the Chief, request forensic and patrol assistance and have an officer meet the ambulance at the hospital to establish a chain of custody and collect the clothes and personal effects for possible trace evidence. The county force was small and underfunded for the area they had to cover, but they'd learned to work with what was available. Sending evidence to the state lab would take weeks, maybe months for results. Scott's family shouldn't have to wait that long. If the autopsy showed poison, or failed to show an obvious natural cause of death, Tucker's investigative skills would be tested.

In the dining room members of the photography group grumbled but shuffled to separate tables. Tucker pulled out a sheet of paper from his pad and handed it to the closest person. "We appreciate your help, and we'll get you out of here as soon as possible. Where was everyone sitting?"

He drew the three tables and the chairs as they were currently arranged in the game room. They passed the drawing to a few people who filled in the blanks. Others crossed off some of those and filled in different names, then the diagram returned to Tucker.

Tucker returned to check out the game room. An incomplete jigsaw puzzle covered a table in one corner. Hundreds of books filled bookcases; DVDs littered shelves. An old fooseball game, a pool table and a ping pong table dominated the far end of the room. A large TV was behind the sheet used as a make-shift screen for the PowerPoint presentation. How many ranch guests had used this room over the years? He took numerous photographs, knowing they wouldn't get much forensic evidence from the well-used room. He concentrated on the three tables used by the group then sealed the room behind him to preserve it for their forensic guy.

Jemma gave Tucker permission to use the ranch office to talk with witnesses. Graves used the front porch. Jemma must have alerted her aunt Alma because no one entered the dining hall from the kitchen. Alma was probably worried about delaying supper for the guests. He'd do his best to clear everything except the game room before the six o'clock supper time.

"Roger, would you like to go first?" At his nod, the two went into the small office next to the dining room.

Tucker shook the judge's hand. He was Tucker's height, a little over six feet, mid-fifties, sixty pounds overweight, and had gray hair at the roots indicating he was overdue for a dye job. Under that good ole boy exterior ran a man whose job had become too routine.

"How's the campaign for re-election going?" Tucker asked as he and the judge settled into two chairs set at an angle to each other near a well-used wooden desk. Tucker dropped a writing pad on the corner of the desk.

"Fair. It's a little early yet. The wife's more excited about it than I am. She loves the dressing up and parties part of the election year. We'll have to invite you to the next one." The judge leaned back and clasped his hands behind his head.

Tucker catalogued the body language as puffing himself up, faking comfort and nothing to hide. "I went to one of your pig pickins last election. You had Elvis sing for us."

"We'll probably book Clinton again this year. He's right fine entertainment." The judge's smile didn't reach his eyes. He probably evaluated Tucker as closely as Tucker did him.

"Tell me something about this photography club."

The judge dropped his hands to his stomach and interlocked his fingers. "It's been around for about five years. I've been a member for two. We usually meet at the Watauga County Library but some other group had signed up for the meeting room in this time slot."

"How did it end up being held here?"

"Jemma Chase volunteered the place. She joined a few months ago."

Tucker nodded slowly. To another investigator, such a scenario could have her setting up for a kill by taking advantage of a setting she knew well. Tucker knew she'd never do anything to harm her family's guest ranch. "You never know about people's hobbies. How'd you get interested in taking pictures?"

"The wife and I took a vacation to the Caymen Islands. When we got back, I realized I'd photographed every sunrise and sunset. Love those brilliant colors. I saw an announcement about the meeting in the paper and decided to keep taking pictures."

Tucker jotted down a few notes, Caymen Islands, bright colors. "How well did you know Scott?"

The judge sat up in the chair, pulled in his legs and rested an arm on the desk. "I wondered how long it would take you to get around to that. He must be dead, and not from natural causes."

Tucker looked down at his notepad then looked back at the judge. Silence many times worked well to get someone to talk. The Chief would want to know every word spoken here.

"I been knowing him for years. His daddy and I were friends at Appalachian State. We've been to a lot of the same events since he's the newspaper reporter-photographer."

"Tell me what happened in there."

"We generally have a business meeting, take a short break, then have a presentation by one of us or a guest speaker. A half hour into the presentation, Scott threw up and started convulsing. Almost hit me with his spewing and I was two chairs down from him."

"Was there anything else different about this meeting?" Sometimes he got more from casual conversation than hard questioning. People saw things without realizing it.

"Not that I noticed. At the break, some of us gathered around Scott to see his Best in Show trophy from a Grandfather Mountain photography contest."

"Some?"

The judge nodded. "Those of us sitting near him. Jemma went to the kitchen earlier to bring out the coffee urn right before the break. I remember because I almost dozed off during the business part of the meeting. The smell of coffee tugged me awake."

"Did you enter the contest?"

"Not this year." A flicker of disgust crossed the judge's face. "My wife forgot to put the application in the mail. By the time I checked on it, the deadline had passed. She's a great woman but sometimes gets too busy with her volunteer work. I'll send in the application myself next year." The judge put his hands on his knees and sat up straight.

Tucker took the hint, figuring he'd ask more questions once he had more information. "Would you mind coming to the sheriff's department tomorrow to sign a statement?"

"Sure. It'll give me a chance to visit the chief. I'll check my calendar and let you know what time."

Tucker followed him out and watched him gather his things and leave before motioning to Tammy Portsmith, next on the list, to follow him to the office. Her handshake was strong; she was small, maybe five-two, athletic walk, forties and not afraid to show her toned upper arms, trim, probably efficient.

"What started you in photography?" he asked as she turned the chair to face him directly before she sat.

"Horses." Her eyes brightened. "Let me show you some of my latest." She reached into her large bag and brought out a slim photo album. She pointed to a black saddlebred.

Thanks to Jemma's influence, Tucker thought he recognized the breed. What he'd learned about horses long ago at his family's farm had faded until Jemma came into his life.

"She's the one I ride most weekends. She's boarding at the stables in Blowing Rock."

"Is this a photo of you?" He looked closely but couldn't tell. The rider wore a helmet and had her back to the camera.

"Yes. A friend took this with my camera. Unfortunately, she waited too long but it shows the ring. I took First in that event. I've been competing at the Blowing Rock Horse Show every year since I moved here four years ago. I've won the last two years and plan to do so again this week."

Add competitive to her list of attributes. "Congratulations. You must be a good rider."

She hesitated, then smiled. Was that from modesty or something else? Tucker pointed to a bag on the floor. "That's a bit big to be lugging around."

Her smile disappeared. "It doubles as an emergency kit, a nurse's occupational hazard. Working in a doctor's office I see all kinds of injuries. I have eye wash in addition to a first aid kit. I like to be prepared." She put away the photo album, zipped closed the bag, and held her hands on her lap.

"What happened in there?" Tucker nodded his head toward the game room.

"Scott won an award and we congratulated him. After the coffee break, he had convulsions."

He paused but she didn't elaborate. "Exactly what did you do before he fell off the chair."

Tammy licked her lips and frowned. "I tried to save him. Everyone will tell you that." Her hands remained clasped on her lap.

Tucker nodded and waited for her to tell the "before" rather than the "after."

"Let's see. I sat a few seats over from him. At break, I stood and stepped over and admired the eight by ten framed photo of a young fawn he held up. I patted him on the shoulder and told him it was a beautiful photo."

Tucker wrote down notes, then looked at her. "Did you enter the same contest?"

"Yes, most of us did. But I didn't win anything. I was happy that one of us won." She kept eye contact with Tucker.

Competitive with horses but not photography? "What did you do next?"

"I went to the bathroom, came out and picked up some coffee and one of those Carolina Delight bars Jemma brought out. She invited us all to come by the ranch any meal time and taste some of her aunt's good cooking. The meeting started again, Aaron began his talk on photographing ghosts. After a while, Leslie yelled 'help'. Scott vomited then went into convulutions. We put him on the floor. He stopped breathing. I checked for pulse and yelled for someone to call 911. I set up the defib Jemma brought and help arrived quickly. I got out of their way." She remained still and composed.

Her recitation sounded as expected, like a nurse's report of facts. "Mind if I see what's in your bag?"

Her face froze momentarily. "I certainly do. No telling what contaminants you have on your hands. What a strange question." The knuckles of her fists turned white.

"The first place trophy is missing." Tucker looked pointedly at the bag. Slow and easy, he reminded himself. Some things can't be rushed.

"I didn't take it. It's probably on the floor somewhere in the game room."

No, but he'd make a point of checking the restrooms. "We'll need for you to come to the sheriff's center and sign a statement." At her nod, he asked her to send in the next person. He jotted down notes, slid the page behind the others and noted the time on a clean sheet of paper. Thunder boomed overhead, and Tucker heard the splash of rain on the roof as the next person came in and shut the door behind him.

"It's a pleasure to meet you, I'm sure. Call me Aaron. Isn't this exciting? And disturbing, of course. I expect Scott will be haunting this place soon." He adjusted the chair a couple of inches to an angle, sat and hung his manbag over the back of the chair. "Now, how can I help you?"

Aaron didn't offer to shake hands, was of medium build, Tucker's height, shaggy brown hair, slight lisp, moved a bit like a girl and was in his mid-thirties. He picked up a paper clip from the desk and threaded it through his long, manicured fingers. His gaze was direct, a hint of a smile at the corners of his mouth.

"Tell me what happened in there." Aaron reminded Tucker of one of his cousins, always well dressed and the girls loved him. They didn't seem to mind that he preferred to date other guys.

"Let's see. The usual group attended, even with the long drive down that dreadful road. Did you notice that everyone is slovenly dressed, with the exception of me and you, of course? City ways are still with me even after two years." He dropped the paper clip and tugged at the collar of his shirt.

"Where are you from?" Couldn't quite place the accent.

"Atlanta. And you?" Aaron dropped his hands to his thighs and rubbed them.

Was he flirting? "I'm from here. What do you do for a living?"

"Getting acquainted questions? How quaint."

Taunting a detective wasn't a good move, Tucker thought.

"I'm a dental hygienist. My dear mother's idea and it has worked out fine for me. Have you always wanted to be a detective?" Aaron's hands were never still. They danced with his words.

Tucker tapped his pen on the note pad. "I'll ask the questions."

"Do forgive me. I'm a better listener than talker. I sat right next to Scott. At break I heard catty Tammy say, 'You'd better enjoy the spotlight now because I'll win next year.' " As if her photography even approaches the quality of Scott's. Her composition is mundane, her knowledge of lighting is … sorry, I'm off track."

"Tell me what you did." Give him something to go on.

"I told Scott why I thought his photo won, then moved aside to hear other comments. I think people like an audience when being praised, don't you?" His question was earnest.

"Go on."

"Harold shook his hand and slapped Scott on the back and almost knocked him down." Aaron's lisp thickened momentarily. "Old army guys have to do the manly thing, don't you know? We both stood there while Summer congratulated him and then I left and went for desert. The delight of oatmeal, chocolate and peanut butter in one bite. You have to try one before you leave. Are you married?"

"No," Tucker answered automatically, distracted by the change of topic. "Are you?"

"Lord no. I only asked because I plan to get a copy of the recipe and was going to give you a copy. You don't look like the type who likes to cook, but you can't go by looks."

"Sometimes they are strong indicators."

"Looks don't tell all. After the break, I started my program. I guess the rest of it won't happen today. It can't go to waste. I'll contact Harold right now and reschedule. Anything else?" He reached behind him for his manbag, prepared to leave.

"I'll need you to sign a written statement. Leave your contact information."

He took a card from a pocket in the bag. "Here's my business card. Call me any time, about anything." Aaron laughed at his own come-on and left.

The rain stopped about the time a square-shouldered man entered the office. The man had a take-charge handshake, was in his seventies, shorter than average, balding.

"What do you want me to do?" Harold asked in a loud voice while dropping into the chair.

Mentally Tucker added "hard of hearing" to his description.

"I took pictures as soon as Scott started having convulsions, even caught him throwing up. Would have videoed it but my digital memory was low so I took a series of stills. Shot the whole room, even you when you walked in the door. I'll send them to you." Harold took off his cap emblazoned with the logo from a Viet Nam unit and set it on the desk.

"If Jemma has her laptop, could we load them onto it now?"

"Glad to be of help." Harold handed over his camera.

Tucker left the room, motioned to Jemma and said in a low voice, "Do you have your laptop with you?"

"In the kitchen."

"Copy these photos, will you?"

"Sure, Gator, anything for you."

Tucker loved that she was as tall as he and watched her long legs walk away too long before turning back to the man in the office. He'd become accustomed to the nickname, short for "investigator," she'd given him. Those were the same words she'd said the other night at his place.

Chapter 2: Monday Afternoon

Poor Scott, Jemma thought, walking into the empty ranch kitchen. Aunt Alma was probably visiting her beau Randy who lived across the road from the ranch entrance. Jemma'd moved her laptop from the game room to the kitchen after calling 911. Hoping no one would notice, she'd taken it away when she'd fetched the defibrillator. Scott's death made her down mood even darker. She'd liked him even though she'd only met him a couple of months ago. The least she could do is help find out what had happened to him. He was only a few years older than she was.

Flirting with Tucker was in poor taste with Scott freshly dead but she had hoped it would lift her spirits. Tucker always dressed his trim body professionally in a tailored shirt, tie, pistol on his hip. His dark hair clipped short, his ready smile deceiving in charm. Their cherished nightly phone conversation would be delayed tonight.

As the official photographer for the ranch, she had all sorts of cables and ports to choose from and had no trouble downloading the file from the camera's memory card. Jemma clicked slide show and watched photos of Harold's real passion before seeing Scott's agony replay through the photos. Her view in real time had been blocked by tables. With each photo, her mood darkened. Harold managed to catch every grim moment from when Scott pushed away from the table and fell on the floor. The convulsions were the worst. The pain he must have gone through while his body bent back on itself.

She copied the files onto a spare stick for Tucker while trying to distance herself from the clear photos she'd just seen. She swallowed bile which had risen in her throat. Another murder in the valley. Reminiscent of stories she'd heard of a murder every Christmas for seven or so years in the 1930s or earlier. Those were fights between two families. This one was unrelated to Triplett Valley. It would have happened in Boone and would have been investigated by town police had the library not rescheduled the meeting room. Fate had delivered another case to her.

If she were discrete and careful, Tucker might let her help. After all, she'd proved to be a valuable resource to him before. First he'd tell her "no" and to keep out of it. He'd remind her that she'd turned down an entry-level job with the law enforcement department and chose to remain a civilian. She'd even cut down on watching the CSI shows she'd taped. Now she only watched one before sleep.

What did she know about Scott? She shut down the laptop, closed the lid, removed the stick, and slid the computer into its case. "The detective wants it kept confidential," she murmured, reinserted the card into the camera and took it back to the office.

***

"Those are for your use only," Harold said to Tucker after Jemma left. "Consider them copyrighted, you understand? Delete the ones on the card of my trophies. You don't need those."

"Trophies?"

"From my hunting trips, some in Africa, Canada, Montana. I sell to hunting, outdoor sports magazines. They like color, action shots. I prefer black and while, makes them grittier. Stark. Like death." Harold slid the camera into a case and put it squarely on the desk.

"You're interested in death?"

"Not in the way you're thinking. Those animals go out in a blaze of glory. Much better than fading away, in my book." Harold rubbed his hands over his chin. "The hunting guides only let us cull out the weak or overpopulated. Limited resources have to be maximally utilized. Can't have the whole population starve to death."

"Does that apply to humans?"

"Why do you think governments and religions invented war? Sterilization would be more humane. I know, political suicide. War is more acceptable. Mind if I stand? Old war injury acts up if I sit too long." Not waiting for Tucker to respond, he pushed back the chair and stood almost "at ease" with his legs spread and his arms behind his back.

"What happened in there?"

"At break, Summer, Roger, the judge and I came over to congratulate Scott. Leslie hung back. She's always last. Some idea that's the way a Southern woman should be.

Polite. Genteel. Never criticizes any of the photos. How can a person get better without a critique from those with knowledge? Just once I'd like to hear her honest opinion." He grinned. "I know she hates the subject of my photos but she finds something positive to say ... framing, clarity and so on."

"After the break, did anything unusual happen?"

"Aaron talked about his ghost photos. All of sudden, Scott spasmed, upchucked and spasmed again. Then you arrived."

Tucker gave him his card and told him to call if he thought of anything else. They'd call him when he needed to report to the sheriff's complex to sign his statement. Tucker followed Harold out of the office. Many of the witnesses had left. He still had two to interview. No sign of Jemma.

"Hello, Summer. How's the family?" Even though he'd known her for years, Tucker consciously viewed her through the potential suspect lens. Thirties, functioning alcoholic, short brown curly hair, regular uniform of golf shirt and khakis, rumor of some steroid use back in her college years on the softball team.

"Everyone's doing good." She followed him into the office, dropped a backpack on the floor, removed gum from her mouth and folded it into a wrapper, then deposited it into her pant's pocket. "And you?"

"Just fine. Are you still with App State?"

"Still teaching in the sports training department. We have some community fitness testing trials going on. Do you want to participate? Pays forty bucks." She looked at Tucker sideways.

"No thanks, but I'll pass the word. Did you go to school with Scott?"

"He was a few years ahead of me at Watauga High but our families go to the same church. Mom will fix some casseroles for his people, I'm sure."

"Did you take any pictures in there?"

"No. I never do. Not like Harold who lives through the lenses. My photos are of people, muscles, shapes, forms. The human body is fascinating." She sat on the edge of her seat, feet flat on the floor, then tapped one foot.

"Did you look at the winning photograph?"

"I'd seen it before but I did give him a quick hug. Lots of people crowded around him." She blinked rapidly and paused, her foot still. In a husky voice she continued. "I'd planned to buy him a drink at Murphy's after the meeting. The effects of the Bloody Mary he always drinks at the meeting would have worn off by then.'

He'd photographed the thermos at Scott's place at the table. "Did you usually go out after a meeting?" At last, someone who would miss Scott.

"Some of us make it a habit. Scott, Aaron, Harold and I were regular about it. Once liquor by the drink passed in August of O8, some of the others joined us. Tammy likes the hard stuff, beer or wine aren't appealing to her. Everyone has joined us at one time or another." Her foot started tapping again.

"Did you see or hear anything out of the ordinary at the meeting?"

"Not that I can think of."

"How about at Murphy's during one of the after meeting trips? Any arguments or confessions that someone may have wished they hadn't said?"

"Probably. Scott was good at that. His main job was photographer but he was also a reporter. He knew everybody. I'll bet he'd talked to or photographed eighty percent of Boone's fourteen thousand people. He wasn't so familiar with the thirteen thousand college students. I work with both populations.

"At Murphy's or elsewhere, did you see or hear anyone threaten him?"

She frowned. "There was once. I hate to mention it because it was months ago. He and the judge got into it. I thought it was an argument about photography styles."

"Specific photographs?"

"Maybe. I was on my third drink and thinking about getting home."

"I'll get this typed up. Stop by tomorrow and sign it. Your office isn't far from the sheriff's complex." He rose and escorted her to the dining area.

"He was a good guy. I'll miss him." Her eyes filled with tears.

Tucker raised his eyebrows.

She half-smiled which spilled a tear down her cheek. "Not in the sense you're thinking. We were friends." She wiped away the tear, grabbed her things and left.

Needing a break from the preliminary interviews, Tucker checked in with the forensics man who already had a box full of bags of evidence. He told Tucker he'd checked the bathrooms, hall and dining room. He'd bagged the contents of the waste baskets but released the rest of the lodge. He'd just started in the game room. Tucker wrote some notes and called in his next witness.

"May I call you Leslie?"

"Please do." She propped her bag on her lap and rested her hands on top. Trim short nails, loose slacks, mid-fifties, blond hair, probably to cover the gray. Shoulders straight, legs crossed at the ankles, a proper Southern lady. "I was a couple seats away when Scott, uh, became ill. We called for help right away. It all happened so fast."

Tucker leaned in to hear her soft voice. "Tell me what happened."

"When we stopped after the business meeting, I commended Scott on his prize but waited until the others had finished. I didn't want to barge up to him, so I waited until most said what they wanted and moved on. After I complimented him on the prize, I went to the sideboard and took a piece of desert and coffee and returned to my place. Jemma asked who wanted copies of a photograph she'd shown earlier. Most of us raised our hands. It was a beautiful scene of some of her horses. She also invited us to dine at her ranch. Wasn't that nice? The meeting started, and Scott took ill, and I called for help."

"What did you think happened?"

"I thought maybe a bee stung him. He's too young for a heart attack."

Bee sting and convulsions? He couldn't see that connection. "Here's my card if you think of anything else. We'll contact you for a formal statement."

Everyone seemed straightforward enough with a few inconsistencies. So far any one of this group could have easily poisoned Scott. It could take weeks, even months to find out what poison was used in the drink. Analysis of Scott's stomach contents could take as long. Motivation would be the key in this case.

People remembered things differently. Usually someone was lying. Maybe all of them lied. Wonder how Graves' interview with Jemma went. Tucker'd caught Jemma in lies before, small ones. He couldn't completely trust her and shouldn't be attracted to her, but he was. Graves said she was good for him, despite everything. Somehow he had to keep her out of this investigation, whether or not she agreed. She opted not to work for the department, and she should honor her own decision. He hated lies and, in his business, he dealt with them every day. Lies hadn't been allowed in his family when he was growing up, and he agreed with that philosophy. Tell the truth, even when it hurt, take the punishment and get on with life. He couldn't figure out how someone kept up with the lies they made up.

Tucker finished interviewing his group about the same time Graves did. The ambulance was long gone; the forensics man would be hours.

"Do you want to stay at the ranch for supper?" Jemma handed Tucker the stick with the transferred photos.

"We have to head back in," Tucker said as Graves walked out the door. When she leaned in, Tucker tightened his jaw for fear she would kiss him good bye in front of someone.

She merely said, "I know you knew Scott. I'm sorry. Call me tonight?"

Jemma could still surprise him. "I doubt it. We'll be late in filing these reports. Catch you tomorrow." He nodded his goodbye, turned and blinked rapidly. Scott had been a good man.

The sun broke through the clouds when Graves drove up the mountain and back across Boone to the sheriff's complex. "Think Jemma will stay out of it and let us do our jobs?"

"You tell me. Did she say anything during your interview?"

"Not much. She said that at the last meeting Scott talked about his big break coming soon while he showed photos of the club members in different places around town. At today's meeting, he said that the first prize was good, but he could top that. When his story was finished, it was his ticket to Charlotte TV reporting. All the other witnesses said pretty much the same thing. Your group sat closer to Scott. Anything there?"

"I had the feeling they all had secrets." Tucker's excitement rose the more he thought about the case. He'd go fishing for the truth and catch the criminal.

"All of my witnesses sounded upset and surprised, even Jemma. Course, I know she didn't do anything. Because of you, she wouldn't dare."

"Since when did you become a trusting soul? No one said anything that tightened your gut?"

"Nothing. I'll check them all out but I think you have the most likely bunch. And, a judge. The luck of the draw. The chief's gonna love this."

The grin on Graves' face notched up the anticipation factor.

Chapter 3: Monday Afternoon

Jemma led three of the members of the photography club to the barn all the while tingling with anticipation of solving another mystery with Tucker. Water droplets on the lush green leaves sparkled like fireflies in the summer sun. Despite Scott's death, these people decided to see the ranch as planned rather than drive back down twisting Elk Creek Road another time. Jemma reminded herself to feed the cats before supper.

The wranglers greeted her in the barn, and she stepped aside to let Visa, Bo's horse, pass by on her way to the pasture. The lower half of the stalls were pine planks with black vertical bars covering the top half. Eight inch wide pine planking reached to the hayloft above the stalls. Floors in the working part of the barn were concrete, with hay covering the dirt floors in the stalls. The whole effect was light and airy despite the iron framing of each stall.

"Enjoy your day off?" Bo hung Visa's tack in the assigned spot on the barn wall.

Jemma shook her head. "Tell you later. Bo, Miguel," Jemma gestured to the crew in the barn, "these are my friends from the photography group, Tammy, Leslie and Harold." Jemma had to admit Bo's chaps, leather hat and Australian riding coat captured the ideal horseman image. No wonder the wrangler tips had doubled this season. Miguel made the most of his straw cowboy hat and a leather vest.

"Heard you might be coming. Miguel and I'd rather be shot by a camera than anything else." Bo drew an imaginary pistol from his imaginary holster and grinned at his own joke.

"Lame, Bo. Tammy's a nurse. She can shoot you pretty quick with a needle. Leslie's a gardener, she's fast with a hose. And Harold's old army, watch out for his pistol." Jemma almost groaned at her own bad quips before leading the group out of the barn and into the pasture. She whistled and Brandy approached. Her brown mare was a long legged, deep chested and smooth-gated horse she'd rescued and turned into a fine saddle horse. Jemma stroked her long neck, keeping mind that she walked with suspects. Imagine planning to poison someone. Think of all the decisions.

"May I shoot your wrangler with a horse?" Leslie asked, fishing the camera out of her bag.

"So long as it's not with a sling." Bo steered Miguel over to Brandy, explaining the by-play.

Brandy became the focus of the impromptu shoot with the wranglers talking and stroking her. While the visitors walked around the pasture taking shots of the mountains, the ranch house and cabins, the barn and the corral, Jemma made sure she took photos of her club friends. She'd print copies and give them as mementos.

"Good horseflesh," Harold said when they returned through the barn. "Wish I could stay for supper but my wife keeps me on a tight rein, if you know what I mean."

Jemma smiled at his old joke. "I hope you two will stay," she said to Tammy and Leslie. After Harold left, she gave the two a tour of the cabins. June was high season so all the cabins were occupied but one guest let them peek inside. Jemma had built some of the beds, hand-hewn the posts. The quilts were old, from her grandmother's collection. Her mom would rather use them for guests than store them away. Jemma led them to the main lodge and told them that she'd see them shortly at supper. The crime scene tape still blocked the door to the game room.

Jemma unlocked her cabin, dually irritated and appreciative of the door lock gift from Detective Tucker. She, like many who lived in the country, didn't generally bother to lock up, but now she had a new habit. As soon as she dropped her camera bag on the table, the cat door clicked and JK and DT rushed in, meowing their greetings. "We have another mystery to solve," she told them while filling their bowls with dry food. "DT, your black undercover fur will be my inspiration in case I have to sneak around. JK, I'll keep your protection instincts in mind." Jemma petted each of them, careful to give equal time and not play favorites.

After locking in the kitties for the night, Jemma sprinted across the yard and rushed in the back door of the ranch kitchen. "Sorry I'm late. What can I do?"

Aunt Alma dried her hands on a kitchen towel. "Wash up. Juanita has everything done. She's only been here two weeks but knows the routine better than you do.

Don't fret. Your heart has always been with the horses instead of near the stove with me."

Whew. She got away with only a mild rebuke. "That's the truth. Juanita, thank you for taking most of the kitchen chores off my hands. I love to eat, don't mind cleaning up but have no talent for cooking."

Juanita took a box from the refrigerator. "You don't care if I take your job?" She divided up wrapped butter pats into bowls for each of the dining room tables.

"Not this part. You have a knack for it." At her puzzled look, Jemma added, "talent, love, interest in cooking."

"Yes. Is easy for me. Sometimes it is fun." Juanita brushed back an errant hair and secured it in her bun.

"Your English is getting better." Jemma liked the young woman, a good ten years her junior and a half a foot shorter than herself.

"Thank you." Juanita fingered the cross on the chain around her neck. "Alma is good teacher."

"How's Alma's Spanish?"

"Not so good," Alma said before Juanita could reply. "She's a better student than I am."

Jemma's gaze slipped past Alma to the counter top by the dining room door. "What have we here?"

"A television, as if you didn't know," Alma held lettuce under the faucet to rinse it.

Jemma followed the coaxle cable cord down the counter, out the door, along the dining room baseboard and under the game room door before returning to the kitchen. She hadn't noticed the cord during the club meeting. She must be slipping. "Who jury-rigged the satellite dish for you?"

"Miguel set up the line for us. Juanita and I wanted to watch the telenovelas in the afternoon but couldn't do that and do all the prep work for supper at the same time."

"Miguel fix the problem, no?" Juanita said, proud of her fiancé.

"Spanish soap operas?"

"Sort of, only they have a thirteen-week story arc with new actors, new plot every season." Alma patted dry the lettuce and tore it into pieces.

"Her Spanish teacher and my English teacher … is a good idea." Juanita pushed the remote control button to un-mute the TV.

Jemma recognized a word or two but couldn't understand the rapid-fire speech of the Latino actors.

Alma glanced up then returned to her work. "Look at those clothes: the bright colors, plus, they have curves. Those women are spitfires. None of those long lingering, over-drawn moments like American soaps. Everything is fast and passionate," Alma said. "Their lover spats are foreplay, an excuse to clear the air and make up."

Jemma stifled a grin. Since her aunt Alma had been dating Randy from across the road, she'd had sex on her mind a lot. "I saw you coming from Randy's late last night. Were you up to no good?"

Alma put her hand on her hip. "Not at all. I tell you it was all good."

Jemma and Alma laughed while Juanita blinked. The joke would have been lost in the explanation.

"On the TV, they like latest fashion," Juanita said. "See those jeans, I can do work like that." She pointed to the colorful embroidery work on the pockets.

Alma glanced at the clock. "I'll wilt these greens before long. You're welcome to join us tomorrow for Spanish lessons. We do my belly dance tape in the early afternoon then watch these telenovelas while setting up for supper."

"Tempting, but I still lead trail-rides most days."

"And Jemma, thanks for getting the police to release my dining room. We could have improvised an outdoor supper but the rain these days has been hard to predict. Plus, that would have made the Wednesday evening cookout less special."

"I didn't have anything to do with it. Tucker moves at his own pace when it comes to investigations."

Jemma left the kitchen with bowls of butter, distributed them to the tables, greeted some of the guests and asked about their afternoon ride along Elk Creek to East Ridge. While they told her about the flock of wild turkeys, she overheard one guest say, "Heard something foreign was in his drink. I'm not talking about the vodka." Another one said, "He was poisoned? Here at the ranch?"

Jemma hurried to her spot at one of the large round dining tables. Wranglers and family members sat at the tables near the kitchen along with her photography club guests. Jemma sat between wranglers Bo and Miguel. Juanita distributed bowls of greens and casserole dishes then sat next to Miguel.

Alma set out plates of roasted deer and settled next her man Randy, who had become a regular dinner guest lately. Tammy and Leslie sat opposite Jemma. As soon as Alma sat, Bo grabbed the closest dish and loaded his plate with meat. Jemma leaned in and spoke quietly to Alma, relaying what she'd overheard.

"We can't have that," Alma said. "You know how people talk. Next thing poisoning'll somehow get linked to my cooking. Jemma, you've gotta do something about this." She lowered her voice even farther. "A nasty rumor like that would break your mother's heart. My brother wouldn't take kindly to it either."

Jemma watched her parents move from table to table, chatting with guests as was their custom. As hosts, their first concern was the comfort and enjoyment of the guests. Truth be told, they got as much of a kick out of making new friends as Jemma did taking pictures. Dad said it was part of the adventure of owning a guest ranch. Each would find an empty chair at a table and share a meal with new found friends.

"What is this?" Bo asked as he passed it to Jemma.

"Venison roast with the sauce from Jane Wilson's cookbook." Alma took some squash casserole and passed it to Randy.

"Tucker told me point blank to stay out of it. You know how the chief is about amateurs interfering in the sheriff's work. I have to leave it to the professionals." Jemma loaded a serving spoon full of squash casserole onto her plate.

"Course you do." Randy dropped some killed lettuce on his plate. "Alma's trying to protect her own. Tucker's a fine detective and will figure this out soon enough. Let's don't make things tougher on the man."

"These vegetables are wonderful, Alma. I'd like the recipe, unless it's a secret." Leslie daintily put another bit of killed lettuce in her mouth.

Jemma put down her fork, suddenly aware she'd been shoveling in her food as if eating were a speed sport. She focused on the conversation.

"Heaven's no. It came from Jane Wilson's cookbook. We don't have secrets around here. Everyone's like family and would find out everything anyhow."

Bo snorted. "If you believe that, I've got this old saddle I'd like to sell you. Already broke in."

Miguel glanced at Juanita.

"Everybody has secrets," Randy said, cutting his eyes over at Alma. "Even you, I reckon."

Alma raised her eyebrows. "I might have tried to get above myself a bit as a girl. Then I got over it. Besides, secrets are like cancer, they take more and more of your energy. Or like leaches, sucking out your spiritual blood."

"How about like kudzu?" Bo looked at Alma for confirmation. "Secrets send out underground runners then blossom and take over everything in their path."

"Good one," Alma said.

"Nah. A guy has to keep a little mystery about him. Otherwise you'd get too comfortable and take me for granted." Randy tucked his head as soon as he said it as if to avoid an imagined blow from Alma.

"Even my cats have secrets. JK hides my braid ties. I've taken to putting them in a drawer." Jemma flipped back her single long braid. Anymore, it migrated to her front when she leaned forward and wouldn't stay hanging down the center of her back like it used to. Maybe she'd changed the way she braided it in the morning.

"Some secrets are better off being kept," Randy said, "especially if they would hurt someone else or bring up something from long ago. What do you think, Leslie?"

"Me? Bless my soul. I don't know. What about you, Tammy?" Leslie looked at Tammy.

Quick to divert attention, Jemma noted.

"I think Randy's right. A little mystery doesn't hurt." Tammy nodded to Randy.

Leslie dabbed the corner of her mouth with a napkin. "Tammy won a trophy last year at the Blowing Rock Horse Show."

"We're always too busy at the ranch to go, but I hear there's some beautiful horses there." Bo waved a fork full of venison as he spoke.

"Not to mention good riding," Jemma added.

"That, too." Bo mumbled while chewing.

"Last year was some tough competition," Leslie said, then smiled at Tammy. "And some scandal about doping a horse. They never found out anything."

Tammy's eyes widened but she kept quiet.

"Tucker would have figured it out but half of the show grounds are in Avery County and they handled the investigation." Bo swallowed his food before adding, "Sorry to hear about Scott. Have you figured out who killed him yet?"

"Stop it, Bo." Jemma put down her fork. "They haven't established why he died. It could have been a heart attack or something. You're feeding the rumors."

"Are you going to follow Tucker's orders and stay out of it?" A twinkle in Randy's eye gave away that he already knew the answer.

Jemma rolled her eyes in response. "What do you think?"

"You're two for two in solving crimes." Bo waggled his empty fork. "You have a reputation to uphold. Can't stop now."

"Quit egging her on, Bo." Alma said. "Tucker's right about letting the sheriff's department do their job."

Juanita looked wide-eyed at Bo then Jemma. "Are you with the police?"

"No, not really. My jobs are to lead trail rides, take photographs and do carpentry work." Jemma glanced at her aunt. "Thankfully, I'm no longer a cook's assistant. I'm not educated enough to do anything else."

"You're still the best amateur detective I know." Bo said.

Jemma wished it were true. While the others ate, Alma and Juanita refilled bowls at the tables to keep the food supplied for the family style dining.

Alma made her announcement about tomorrow's events. "At nine, riders leave for the Tail Feather Cove ride and then leave at two for the Racoon Run ride.

"Non-riders meet at one to go to the Banner Elk Winery. As an added bonus, you'll have a winery tour with the owners, Dick Wolfe and his wife, DeDe. Dr. Wolfe wrote a book, *Climbing Kilimanjaro at 70,* about his adventure. He celebrated his January birthday on the slopes, then completed the climb. Amazing man. The Chase's had dinner at the winery last week. That's a treat you should all schedule next time you're in the mountains."

After supper, Jemma walked over the spring fed stream to return to her cabin and added dry cat food to JK & DT's bowls. She removed a hammer and dusty tool belt from her desk in the corner of her living room, disturbing some old papers in the clutter of her desk. One stopped her thoughts … a sketched layout of her planned remodel of the upstairs.

Her cabin was originally built in 1901 with outdoor plumbing. Someone over the years had added a bathroom downstairs and a toilet and sink upstairs. She'd finished her downstairs remodel last year, but stalled on working on the upstairs.

The cabin belonged to her parents, as did everything else on the ranch, but they'd given her permission to remodel any way she wanted. They were just happy to have her back home with them.

She settled down before her computer and checked Tammy's Facebook page where she was linked with most of the photography club members. Blog pieces of horses, shows, competitions and training filled Tammy's pages along with a few connections to nurses. Her divorce hadn't been amicable. Jemma followed Tammy's trail to other online sites and mentally built a stronger history of the lady. She printed some pages and cleared a spot on the desk for this new investigation.

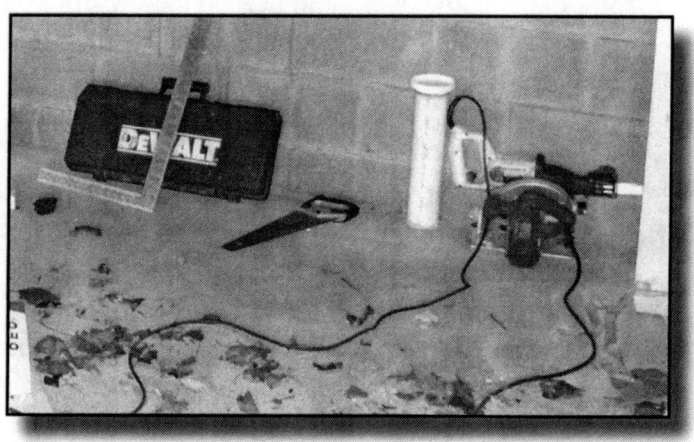

Chapter 4: Monday Evening

Tucker took a deep breath and slowly released it before ringing the Barker's doorbell. Graves stood a little behind him. He'd called the hospital and confirmed Scott's death. When Scott's mother opened the door, her welcoming smile faltered when she looked at Tucker's face.

"I'm sorry," he said.

"Something's happened to my Scott." Her hands flew to her heart.

Scott's father came up behind her. "What's wrong?"

Tucker swallowed hard. "It's about Scott. He died this afternoon."

"What? How? Are you sure?" Mr. Barker put an arm around his wife.

"I wish it weren't true, but he's gone." Tucker waited, to give them a few moments. "Would it be possible for me to ask a few questions?"

Mrs. Barker cried into her husband's chest.

Tucker glanced back at Graves, still absorbing the knowledge he would never again run into Scott at ball games, the Boone Drug lunch counter or gathering information at an accident.

Mr. Barker looked up while still holding his wife close. "Was it a car accident? Did he hurt anyone else?"

"No. At this point, he died of undetermined causes. Do you know of anyone who would want to harm Scott? His ex-wife? Anyone?"

"Come in. Sorry about my manners," Mrs. Barker said, wiping her eyes and leading them to the living room.

Tucker and Graves sat on a worn sofa facing the couple he hadn't seen in years. Mr. Barker's arm was around his wife who tried to stop crying but finally let the tears flow. Tucker blinked to keep back tears but gave up. He cried along with her, and soon Mr. Barker allowed himself the release. Graves sat quietly and waited.

After a while, Mr. Barker asked Tucker to repeat the question. "No, she moved to California. His girlfriend lives in Charlotte. He was working on a big story he hoped to parlay into a job offer from a television station there."

The living room tables were cluttered with framed family photographs, mementos and books. The walls held photographs, some he recognized from the newspapers. "Do you know what the story was about?" Tucker took a deep breath and forced himself to focus again on finding the motive—if it proved to be intentional poisoning.

Mr. Barker shook his head slowly. "We talked to him last night but he didn't mention it. He didn't like to tell anyone about his work, some crazy idea that it would spoil the energy of the story. He preferred to get others to talk. What happened to him?"

"He was at a photography club meeting down in Triplett and died during the meeting. We don't yet know why. What was his medical history?"

"He was fit. Drank too much but talked about cutting back. No heart disease in the family. He wasn't on any medication. He ran at the Greenway park regularly." Mr. Barker swallowed hard.

They needed time to absorb the loss. Tucker gave them his card and asked them to call if they thought of anything else. Mrs. Barker hugged him before they left. Tucker figured his own parents would react in a similar fashion if something happened to him. The difference was that Scott's profession was supposed to be less risky than his own.

Graves went home and Tucker returned to the office. Later that evening after Tucker set up Alerts on each of the suspects and Scott for his computer inbox, Tucker stopped by Mindy's for a burger and found a table by the window. He'd done all he could until tomorrow. Sleep could bring answers; at least it had helped in the past. Think of something else.

French fries and ketchup deserved his undivided attention. Maybe the fifty sit-ups and push-ups he did every morning helped to counter this once a week treat. Too bad the county couldn't afford an on-site gym like the fire departments had. He stuffed four fries into his mouth flooding his tongue with salt and fat. Jemma would be surrounded by family and guests, he thought, while he, once again, ate alone. Maybe he should get in the habit of driving down that mountain to see her during the week instead of his own rule of making that trip only on weekends. It was only a half hour drive. He did want to be around her and didn't want to become an old bachelor, as Graves had called him. Not that just north of forty was old.

Scott had saved his reputation once, back when

Tucker was fairly new on the job and in his mid-twenties. Tucker had run into the downtown Boone Drug store one morning to pick up something, maybe band aids for his mom. The regulars sat in booths or on stools around the lunch counter. Lawyers, school board members, real estate builders and sellers—some of the local power brokers had breakfast together almost every morning. The model train ran overhead around the dining section even then.

Scott worked the counter during the summer break in high school and butted in on a conversation. "That's not true. I know for a fact that Tucker would never be at a cockfight. He's built like my cousin who was there and dumb enough to brag about it." Tucker never forgot what was probably a minor incident to Scott. Being falsely accused could have haunted his career, especially if it involved cruelty to animals. He'd thought about thanking him one day but couldn't figure out what to say without sounding foolish. If his death was murder, finding the killer would have to be his thanks.

Tucker took a full bite of his burger when he saw a woman walking his way that he never expected to see again. Wanda looked at him, smiled and approached with her tray.

"Mind if I join you? I wondered if you were still around here." Her mountain twang had developed into a vocal melody.

Tucker nodded, chewed fast, swallowed his food, then swallowed again as he stood. Her hair was shorter, her clothes more refined, her speech faster.

"How have you been?" Brilliant opener, he thought, sitting after she sat. Some things didn't change.

"Good. I'm in the pet store business and thinking of

opening a branch in Boone. How about you?" Wanda emptied her tray and put it on a vacant table. She unfolded her napkin and placed it on her lap before taking the lid off her salad.

Tucker found himself absorbed in her every move. "I'm good." He shook his head then decided to ask as soon as the question popped into his mind, "How's your husband?"

She smiled, showing off bright white teeth. "Long gone. We split up ages ago and I've focused on business in Charlotte. I'll be in town for a week." She opened a dressing packet and poured half on her salad. "What do you do? Are you married?"

"No. I'm a detective for the sheriff's office."

She nibbled at her salad. "Did you find anyone to replace me?" She laughed at the stunned expression Tucker tried to cover.

Her laugh stirred a memory. Summer on a trail off the Blue Ridge Parkway, a blanket, a bottle of cheap champagne. "You're one of a kind, Wanda. We were young, in our early twenties, a crazy time for most people." He gulped down some water.

"I never forgot you. I often wonder what could have happened." Wanda tilted her head and half closed her eyes.

Tucker glanced at neighboring tables. Most were empty at this hour. "You were married," he said quietly. "We should have been stronger and resisted."

"I don't regret a thing." She looked straight at him. "You were the best thing in my life at that time. My ex was not a bad man, just a boring one. Too bad I didn't figure out my life until after we moved away."

Tucker and Wanda ate in silence for a few moments as

Tucker tried to keep memories from flooding his mind. He concentrated on eating every french fry, reluctant to let the time with her end. "You taught me a thing or two. You introduced me to a few moves I'd never imagined."

"It was fun ... the thrill of sneaking around, of snatching moments." She paused to study her salad. "With you working a job and studying to graduate from ASU, we had to be very inventive with our little bits of stolen time."

She's flirting with me, he thought, and shook his head. "My one taste of being naughty. I've behaved since then."

"That's a shame. We could make up for lost time this week." She leaned back in the chair and raised an eyebrow.

"Tempting, but no. I'm seeing someone." His heart beat faster, thinking of Jemma, he told himself.

"All the better. You would get the thrill of hiding something, a reversal of roles." She covered the rest of her salad and collected her trash. "Come, walk me to my car."

Tucker deposited the trays and trash and followed her out into the well-lit parking lot. She pressed the unlock button on her keys and leaned back against the BMW, pulling him close. "For old time's sake," she whispered and then kissed him thoroughly on the lips. Despite himself, a thrilling current flowed through his body and he slipped his hands behind her neck. Time and experience dropped away, he was in his twenties again. Life was fresh and optimistic. A beautiful woman wanted him right now.

A car horn beeped and he broke the kiss, shocked at himself. What about Jemma?

Chapter 5: Tuesday Morning

First thing, Tucker and Graves stood before the chief's desk in the new Watauga County Law Enforcement Center. File cabinets lined one wall; another wall held two windows with one-way glass so she could observe the two interrogation rooms. Considering the current high case load of her investigators, her desk was neat. Not only was she good with keeping her investigators on track, she also kept victims and their families up to date with progress and kept the sheriff informed.

"We're going on the assumption of poison until the autopsy and toxicology reports come back." She closed the Scott Baker file on her desk. "Solve it fast. Poison at Blue Falls Ranch has all of Triplett Valley in alarm as well as the other Watauga County communities. Scott Baker was a respected reporter. He deserves our best. What else do you have?" She tapped the file.

"Photos taken by one of the club members as Scott died." Copies would be added to the file later today.

The chief shook her head with a wry smile. "What else?"

"We've split the suspects since there are so many.

Most of them will be in today with statements."

"I see by your notes your friend, Jemma Chase, was there. Who talked with her?"

"Graves did."

The chief nodded her relief.

"I don't see how I need to be disqualified from the case. He can take her statement and leave me out of it. Besides, Scott was a friend."

She studied him steadily. "Will she stay out of it? Tucker, you would have to guarantee she won't do any investigating on her own. She could be hurt. Can you do that?"

"I'll do my best." Why would Jemma stifle her SCI wannabe bent now when she wouldn't do so before?

"Your job may be on the line this time. At the least, you will be pulled from the case. Do you understand?" She jotted notes as she spoke.

"Yes, ma'am." Tucker said on his way out and stopped by his desk. Jemma would be a problem. Maybe more so this time than when they first met. Back then he and Graves had interviewed her at the old sheriff's office and jail. The cinder block building had cramped small offices located down the hall past the jail cells. This place had a big room with an individual cubical for each detective. Eye to eye contact took seconds instead of a phone call and a walk through the old labyrinth.

"How much coffee did you have?" Graves asked on his way to his own desk.

"Two. Why?"

"You're prancing like an eager horse before a race. Bet you spent most of the night thinking about this case."

Tucker felt the muscle at the corner of his mouth twitch. "And you didn't?"

"My wife helps me put this stuff in perspective."

"I'll take Interview Room One, you can have Two." Tucker phoned his witnesses and set up interview times.

"Thank you for coming in right away, Summer." Tucker led her to the interview room down the long hall.

"I have time between classes."

Tucker opened the metal door and let her enter the eight by ten room first. He closed the door quietly while her gaze darted around the room. She shivered even though the whole building was kept at seventy-two degrees in the summer.

Summer slid onto the metal bench against the wall. "Scott was a friend. He was easy to talk to. My parents and I spent the evening praying for his soul. Far as I know, he never hurt anyone. His sins were more self-destructive like drinking. His reporting always took families into account."

Tucker moved his chair to the end of the table so he sat closer to her to keep the talk informal but mindful of the camera in the upper corner behind him. "You were about twelve when your parents turned from the commune to the Baptist Church, weren't you?"

"If you're asking if I remember what they were like before finding religion, yes I do. That was eighteen years ago. I'm happy for them. It's not the life I've chosen but I'm respectful of their beliefs." She hunched her shoulders and slipped her hands under her thighs.

"Do you think anyone ever told Scott too much at Murphy's?" Likely she hid something from her parents. At thirty, she ought to be coming into her own.

"Like I said, he was easy to talk to. I'm sure people told him things he didn't print. Little sins." She chewed her lower lip. "He was holding out for that one story that would get him noticed in Charlotte. He was ready for a job at a bigger place. Part of him was restless." She squeezed her eyes shut. "Sorry, I promised myself not to cry."

Tucker waited until she opened her eyes. "Do you want to do this another time?"

"No. I want to help."

"Did he find the story?"

"I don't know. I wished it for him, but now, I hope it didn't cause all of this. What if I said or did something that pointed to Scott and caused someone to want to stop a story?"

So much for keeping the poison angle out of the picture. "I understand he drank during the club meetings."

"All the time." Summer released her hands and placed them on the table. "He said that Bloody Mary's gave him a full serving of vegetables and made him feel less guilty about drinking. He made a batch fresh every day and brought it in a car coffee mug, one of those with a screw on top. He'd set it down, take off the lid and sip on it all through the meeting."

"Where did you sit yesterday?"

"Right next to Scott. I usually did since I've known him so long." Her eyes teared up but she didn't cry.

"Did you see anyone come near his drink?"

Her eyes widened. "So he was poisoned. That's terrible. I didn't notice anyone but it could have happened easily enough when we congratulated him on the contest. You think one of us killed him?" Her mouth dropped open. "Me?"

"Calm down, Summer. I'm just asking questions." He sat back in his chair and tapped his notebook, then glimpsed himself in the two-way mirror. All interviews were taped but not all were monitored in real time by the chief.

Summer sat up straight, took in a breath and let it out slowly. "We're scheduled to finish the meeting tomorrow night at Aaron's house. We'll be talking about evil … to use my parents' words."

"Like what?"

"Haints. Ghosts. Aaron says he's taken a photo of the one in his house. A part of it was built way back in the 1890s."

Tucker nodded. He knew the house; everyone still called it the Wilson house, even though no one named Wilson had lived in it for as long as he remembered.

"Look over this statement and let me know what you want changed." Tucker liked Summer and thought it would be a shame if she had something to do with Scott's murder. She didn't give him much he didn't already know. A dribble or two. Despite her sadness over Scott, she remained on the suspect list. Sometimes the guilty ones were the most emotional. After she signed the statement, he walked her out and brought in Harold.

"What did you think of my photographs? I looked them over last night. They were clear, action shots. I did a good job." Harold talked in clipped tones while sliding onto the bench. He placed his cap on the table, sure to set the military logo emblazoned on the bill toward Tucker.

"Yes, you did. One of the detectives is working with them now. We appreciate your help. Any idea who would want to harm Scott?" Tucker moved the chair and sat on the other side of the metal table.

"He was a reporter. His job was to find out secrets and use them to make a good story. He stirred up a lot of folks. One time he did a story on my trophies, a lion I bagged in Africa. That created an uproar in the community." Harold's eyes took in the two-way mirror, the camera in the upper corner and the metal rings to secure a prisoner to the bench he sat on. "We've got people who hunt deer out of season all over the county, but no one talks about that. I paid good money to hunt legally in another country and they write letters to the editor complaining. I helped support a village with that African hunt."

"Were you mad at Scott for that article?"

"Mad? No. The reaction confirmed my opinion that people raise an alarm when it's not their family. Every man out there has a gun collection and fights to defend the right to bear arms. They'll turn around and cry when I cull an animal. Where do they think their steak comes from? At least that tiger ran free and lived a relatively long life."

"Were you army?" A question designed to steer Harold away from politics.

Harold straightened his shoulders. "For thirty years. I'm too old to be recalled to duty but would love to go if they'd have me. Best years of my life. The wife is happier now that we don't move every few years."

He seemed eager to be heard, to voice his opinions. Bet he was a news junkie who talked back to the TV anchor. His wife'd probably tuned him out years ago. "Do you have anything to add to this statement?"

Harold looked it over and shook his head. "Poison's a woman's weapon. I'll bet Summer has some secret. I've smelled alcohol on her breath a time or two. Another thing, the way she looks at other women makes me think she's in that 'don't ask, don't tell' category. You should check with Aaron, too. Rumor has it that Scott turned him down. He's in the same category, if you know what I mean." Disquiet squinted his eyes.

"What makes you think it was poison?"

"I was a medic for a while in the army. I'd say someone slipped a mickey into his drink during the break. It would have been easy to do. Did you check his laptop? It was one of those electric blue minis. He carried it with him everywhere. Some of us bring ours to meetings to show our latest work."

"I'll look into it. Thank you for your help. Here's my card if you think of anything else." Tucker showed him out, relieved to finally have some excuse for action. Interviews were important but physical evidence called to him.

Tucker didn't remember seeing a laptop in the photos he'd hastily looked at. It wasn't in Scott's car yesterday. Tucker checked the other Interrogation Room, and it was empty so he returned to his desk and found Graves finalizing the statements. Tucker called the Barkers and received permission to search Scott's apartment and anything else that would help the investigation. Tucker and Graves drove to the apartment complex, not much different from the surrounding student apartments.

Scott had lived alone, and the place had that bachelor feel of utilitarian brown furniture, plastic plates and miss-matched glasses. The ex-wife had taken anything of value since it hadn't mattered much to Scott. His interest was in the story and the pictures, not in how he lived. Half a dozen empty vodka bottles hugged a recycling bin in the kitchen corner. Empty tomato juice cans filled a second bin. Frozen dinners were stacked in the freezer. A quick look in the refrigerator revealed a lone bottle of water, dated months ago. This was not a home but merely a place to sleep and store his pictures. Scott's life had been the hunt, the job and a search for a better future.

Hundreds of photographs were stacked in cardboard file boxes. The boxes were labeled by topic, rather than date. Tucker figured many were duplicates of the newspaper files. Hand labeled CDs spilled over a file box and onto the desk. Tucker looked at a few, realizing they contained thousands more photos. He glanced through Scott's mail, piled haphazardly on the kitchen table.

The bedroom was sparse; clothes hung up, laundry in a hamper. Scott had made a half-hearted attempt to make his bed. Clock, lamp, notepad, pen and a photograph of a woman covered a bedside table. Scott's parents had called his girlfriend, saving Tucker that duty. The bathroom held one toothbrush and no girly bath gels. Looked like he visited her more than she visited him. Tucker returned to the living room.

"Look at this," Graves said, handing Tucker a desk calendar. "He'd met most of our suspects at Murphy's at one time or another during the past month."

Saving it for last, Tucker booted up Scott's home computer and clicked on the icon for stories. It listed stories sold, how much paid, stories out for consideration. "We'll take this in and have the tech guys monitor his emails, social networks. We might get something out of those. If we're lucky, these files held the same secrets as his missing mini laptop."

Chapter 6: Tuesday Morning

Jemma inhaled the moist summer air tinged with saddle oil and Brandy's familiar odor. She signaled Brandy to walk to today's trail. Jemma pretended to be enthusiastic about the ride as she motioned for the guests to follow her lead.

They left the tinkling babble of the creek. The trees still had a mix of light and dark green leaves, not yet into the uniform deep greens of late summer. The sixty degrees would warm to the mid-seventies by noon. Many riders wore jackets. Even the relief of fine weather didn't lift her spirits.

Something besides Scott's death yesterday kept her down. She felt like a drudge, a drone, another cog in a wheel. Nothing special about her. No high paying job. She worked three menial jobs. Nothing she did mattered.

The horses and riders settled in behind her on the picturesque ride to Tail Feather Cove. Tuesday rides were a notch harder than the Monday rides but both were easy on the wranglers. Horses were herd animals and liked to follow a lead mare. According to an ebook she'd downloaded on a whim because the title, Horses Teaching People, caught her eye, horses were negative reinforcement animals and responded when the pressure was released or when the attention wandered and they had their own lead. Unlike people and dogs who responded to positive pressure. Horses supposedly had the ability to balance people who were depressed. Jemma rubbed Brandy's neck. Why wasn't it working for her?

Jemma turned in the saddle for a moment and saw Miguel in the middle of the line pointing to the slack reins a rider had neglected. Miguel had improved his English greatly since last year, his first at the ranch. He still understood much more than he spoke, but he was getting used to helping riders keep their horses in line. They all avoided too much talking since spotting a deer in the woods was the goal of most of their guests. Some wanted to see a brown bear but that wasn't on Jemma's list. Bears had been spotted in the valley in recent years but had so far avoided the ranch.

Aunt Alma was careful about storing food and table scraps to keep the critters away. So far the wildcats remained up on their ridge. Still, having the bunkhouse within earshot of the stables had been good planning on her father's part.

Brandy's sure footed rhythm allowed Jemma's thoughts to ramble. Despite yesterday's rain and their once-a-week ride on this trail, the ground remained hard packed. Little bluets and tiny wild strawberries lined the trail for a short ways. The broad shiny leaves of low growing galax could be spotted in the woods. The tall, straight poplar trees swayed with the gentle summer breeze.

Two hours on Brandy some days was a quiet riding meditation; on others, she had to pay constant attention to the guests. The dynamics varied from group to group. These guests were better riders than most. They'd want to gallop before the day was out.

Poor Scott. What could he have possibly done to deserve silencing like that? The killer knew Scott's habit of bringing his own shot of vodka, his own poison in a way, to the club meetings. We all did.

It was a bold act, poisoning in a large group of people. Any one of us could have done it. How long could it take to drop something into the Bloody Mary? Scott always stirred it before taking a drink, to mix up the fire from the hot sauce, he said. That talk last month about his big break into broadcast news must have triggered something. What were some of those photos he showed us? He'd photographed ninety percent of us.

Tammy's fleeting frown when Leslie mentioned the doping at the horse show might be important. As a nurse, she wouldn't be squeamish about giving a shot to a horse. She knew horses and could easily find out how to knock one off its stride with an injection in the right place. Horse shows were even more crowded than yesterday's meeting. She could have wanted to win at any cost. It wouldn't have permanently harmed the horse. Had Scott photographed her doing something illegal? Had she put the horse medicine into his drink and killed him? Jemma rubbed Brandy's neck and turned to check out the line behind her. Bo brought up the rear, riding close behind the last guest to keep the group together.

They'd been following Elk Creek down to Tail Feather Cove where the land owners had let the ranch set up log benches in the bend in the river. Lush ferns hugged the rocky ground. The creek water still ran a milky brown from the hard rain, which, she thought as she looked up, might continue later that afternoon. They circled around and Jemma had everyone dismount for a few minutes of rest and picture taking.

"Look at you," Bo said.

Jemma bristled at the scorn in his tone, looked down and didn't see anything out of the ordinary.

"I know we want to be casual and rustic but a stained workshirt? What's that from?"

"Leather polish. Or do you mean the mustard?"

"You make me wear this get up then you look like that?" Bo poked back his cowboy hat.

Jemma tried to wipe off the stain from her shirt. How had she let herself go? When had she stopped caring about how she looked? Months ago when she'd turned down the legitimate job of working for the sheriff's department. That was it. Over the winter she'd regretted it when carpentry work was slow and tourist season had presented few sales of her photographs. Menial jobs were all she was qualified to do. Why did she turn down a relatively prestigious one where she could dress better every day for an office job?

Solving this new mystery would raise her spirits, she promised herself. She would save the valley's reputation and be a hero, be someone worthwhile. She'd reinforce her reputation and pull herself out of this slump.

"Let's head back," she said to the wranglers.

At the ranch for lunch, she called Tucker from the check-in desk phone, wishing yet again that cell phones worked in the valley. "What can you find out about the Blowing Rock Horse show poisoning last year?" She tried to brush off the mustard spot on her shirt, sure it wasn't a stain.

"Why?"

"Tammy may have been involved. Scott could have been on to her." She stopped fussing with her shirt, expecting excitement about her clue.

"Thanks for the tip. Now don't get mad at this, but you have to stop. The chief has told me that I could lose my job if you start snooping around. She doesn't want you to get hurt. Let me do my job."

"But—"

"She's right. Tell me all the ideas you have and let me investigate. Don't keep anything from me. You know how I hate it when you don't tell me everything. You named me Gator, right?"

The firm coaxing in his voice deflated Jemma. "I did. You will check up on Tammy?"

Blocked from being a hero? How unfair that a murder happened in front of her and she couldn't help.

"I will. Gotta go."

Searching for sympathy, Jemma went to the ranch kitchen and told Alma. Alma understood her, knew her penchant for galloping into a problem and concocting possible resolutions.

"He's right. You could be put in danger … again."

No, this couldn't happen. Alma against her, too. Jemma clenched her jaw and swallowed her argument. Alma was her respected aunt, after all.

"What do you need that for? Let him have the glory. Stick to helping out here and taking your pictures. When are you going to fix this cabinet door? I asked you to do it last week. While you're at it, throw away that shirt. You look like you shovel manure for a living."

Chapter 7: Tuesday Morning

Tucker checked the newspaper archives online concerning the Blowing Rock horse doping, printed the articles, had the Blowing Rock Police fax their report, and put everything in a folder. Ticking in the back of his mind was his kiss with Wanda and that Jemma wouldn't like it. He led Aaron to the interrogation room.

"Oh, Detective, I hope this doesn't take long. I have to get the house ready for company Thursday night. I'll finally present my ideas about photographing ghosts to the group. My program was delayed by poor Scott's demise." He put his manbag on the metal bench then scooted in.

"What's the hurry?"

Aaron paused and looked around the room. "Functional, I suppose. Oh, I'm submitting an article to Photo-Play and want the group's opinion before I send it in. Something about the piece isn't quite right. Besides, after the funeral would be too depressing."

"Do you have anything to add to this statement?" Tucker slid the paper across the metal table top.

He scanned the page. "I sat next to him and didn't see anything unusual. Convulsions. Ugh. What a way to go." He signed and handed the page to Tucker. "I hope to go in my lover's arms. Don't you? Something romantic about the ultimate last gasp while making love. Oh, my mother would slap my face for saying something like that. She's in Atlanta, thankfully. I love my momma but she doesn't need to know everything, right?" He grabbed the strap to the bag and started to get up.

Tucker decided to take Aaron's hint and let the interview end but seized the opening for one last question. "Did, uh, were you ever romantically involved with Scott?"

"Why do you ask?" He stood and straightened his pants. "Oh, am I a suspect? How lovely." He smiled and his eyes lit up as if he'd discovered a treasure. "I can't wait to tell Mother. She'll think it's rich. Detective, I never kiss and tell." He waved goodbye and opened the door. Aaron had been too breezy and determined to control the interview. Let him run. Tucker could always reel him back in. Jemma'd fill him in on the ghost session.

Tucker followed Aaron to the door and leaned in the corner as Aaron left. He heard Aaron say, "Your turn, Tammy. That's a pretty handbag. Is it new?"

Ignoring his question, she whispered, "How was it? Was he tough?"

"Not as tough as you, sweetheart. Unless you have something to hide. Anything I should know about?"

She swatted him on the arm and entered the interview room, nodding when she saw Tucker.

"Do you like working in a doctor's office?" Tucker asked, pointing to where she should sit.

"Yes. It's too busy sometimes but nothing like working in a hospital. My doctor's a good man who genuinely cares about his patients. And I have regular hours which are flexible enough for me to get time off for things like attending the photography club meeting." Tammy clasped her hands on the table.

"Tell me again about Scott." Would she be consistent? Would she be too detailed or go off on a tangent?

"At the break, he was fine. Shortly after Aaron began his talk, Scott started gasping for air then went into convulsions. I haven't had much experience with poison, but I'd say he was given a big dose. I feel inadequate that I couldn't help him." Her hands remained clasped; her tone, even.

Had everyone concluded it was poison? "By all accounts, it was a nasty way to go. What do you think it was?"

"My guess would be strychnine. Many times the victim survives the first set of convulsions only to have another one in fifteen to twenty minutes. Not this time. You'd have to consult a poison expert to be sure."

Her objectivity irritated Tucker. Scott had been a friend. "Where would one get the stuff?" Tucker leaned back and tapped his pen on the table.

"You'd have to look that up online. There may be natural plants that cause the body to react the same way. I'm only guessing since I don't know much about it. My job is to save someone, not kill them." She slid back on the bench and flattened her back against the wall.

He pointed the pen at her. "I understand you won a trophy at the Blowing Rock Horse show last year. Congratulations."

Tammy turned to the side at the end of the bench, crossed her legs and clasped her hands in her lap. "I trained hard to win. Thank you."

"It must take a lot of practice to get that good." Tucker looked for guilty knowledge micro expressions and saw one as she licked her lip. He leaned in and rested his elbows on the table in an effort to seem friendly.

"I'm at the stables every chance I get." Her voice softened.

"You're a regular face out there. Everyone knows you. So much so you've become a fixture, wouldn't you say?"

She blinked twice. "I do know all the boarded horses, if that's what you're getting at."

"All the competitors, their quirks. You've studied them. I understand you video the elimination rounds and practice sessions."

She turned to squarely face him. "I'm not the only one. Is there something wrong to want to win? I'm competitive. It gives me the push to improve."

"Where's the trophy?"

"From the horse show? In my living room." Tammy crossed her arms over her chest. "Or it will be. I have to win three years in a row to keep it."

He'd hoped she'd slip and think of Scott's photography award trophy. No luck this time. "Please read this statement and let me know if you have anything to add." He needed more time to investigate her further. No sense in alerting her now.

After she left, Tucker and Graves took over one of the conference rooms. Tucker taped up photos for each of the six suspects on the left side of the rolling board and one of Scott on the right. Under each photo, he taped a piece of legal paper listing in black marker the suspect's name, job, type of photography. "What do we know about Harold?" Tucker asked.

"Former military, likes hunting, likes black and white photography."

"No nonsense man. More likely to shoot someone than poison one. Happily married?"

"So he says, according to your notes. We need to check with some neighbors. Motivation?"

"Caught in the act of something? Girlfriend? Poaching? Maybe something in his military record he wants to keep secret. You take him," Tucker said, pulling from his pocket a toy soldier he'd taken from a memento box he looked through before leaving that morning. He placed it on the table near Graves.

Tucker moved to Aaron's column. "Import from Atlanta, single, gay reputation, photographs women like he wishes he were one, chats like one anyway. A dental hygienist meets all kinds of people. He could have cleaned Scott's teeth and blurted out something. Claims to have left Atlanta because it was too hot. He could use poison. Scott could have found out about too many ejaculations or into the wrong person. I'll check up on him." Tucker put an old tooth brush on the table.

"I'll take Tammy," Graves said. "She's high on your list and it'll keep the whole investigation balanced. Nurse, imported four years ago after a nasty divorce. Poison isn't that far from injections, which she's used to. My guess she turned to horses as a man substitute. You think she was caught doping the top contender's horse so she could win last year." Graves held out his hand for the next item.

"Sorry. That was all I could come up with this morning. Doesn't that same horse show kick off on Thursday? Work on her file first." Tucker tapped the photo of Leslie. "Is that the best one we have?"

"She doesn't like to have her picture taken."

"Leslie wants to be a grandmother, likes to garden, photographs flowers, devoted wife and mother. Takes photos, too many of them according to Scott's notes. Even keeps the bad ones. What could she be hiding?"

"Pesticides. Maybe Scott photographed her using a banned substance. Better yet, raising marijuana. ASU students would be a big market for dope. She could have a basement devoted to the plants complete with grow lights and humidity control."

"Right. I'll take her. Our drug division may have something on her. We can check for electricity usage as well as water usage. Since she's within the town limits, she won't have a well." Tucker didn't believe she was a serious contender, but kept an open mind.

He moved to the next photo. "I know Sunny better than you do so you take her. Single, sports trainer, drinks too much, probably a functioning alcoholic. Also photographs women, but hers are athletes. She'd use poison. Scott could have photographed her drunk or with someone in a compromising position. She loves that job and would do anything to protect it."

"That leaves the judge. Married to the same woman for over thirty years, supports the community, photographs sunsets and fires. Tried too many times to run for a state office and finally gave up last year. Scott could have had something to do with that. He has lots of secrets, I expect, since he's been in law for so long. Personal secrets?"

"Women? Men?"

"It does come down to money, sex or power. I'll take him." Tucker turned around the rolling board in case anyone else wanted the conference room.

***

"Bo, sure you'll be okay with the horses?" Jemma had just unsaddled Brandy after the Racoon Run afternoon ride.

"Go. I'll put the guests to work brushing down their own horses." Bo turned to the guest riders and asked for volunteers. "It's for a good cause. Miguel wants to give his fiancé a surprise gift."

Half of the guests took Bo up on the request so Jemma and Miguel left. After a stop at Jemma's cabin for tools, Jemma's tool belt and a package which was delivered the day before, they slipped in the front door of the lodge, watching for Juanita who was supposed to be busy in the kitchen helping Alma prepare the evening meal.

They quickly crossed the open two-story lofted space, relieved that the dining room was empty. Directly opposite, the "Do not cross" police tape was gone from the game room doorway. Jemma held her index finger to her lips, signaling her mom at the check-in desk that they were on a secret mission.

Miguel led the way up the stairs, took a left, passed by a "signed by Jemma" framed photograph of the local waterfall to a short hall on the right which held doors to four rooms. He unlocked the first door on the left and motioned Jemma inside. He flipped on the light and frowned at her before closing them in. "Do you think she saw us?"

"No, but we need to be as quiet as possible. The corner of the kitchen is below us. Let's put down our tools further in the room. That way we'll be over the dining room and less likely to be heard." Jemma set down the jig saw and the package then spread a collecting cloth on the floor on the closet side of the centered ceiling fan. Although there was a window in this interior room, it overlooked the walk around the lofted entry and did not offer natural light.

"Juanita did not mean to complain about this room you gave her." Miguel tugged the cloth straight.

'It was a store room with no light. I had hoped adding the window would be enough, but she's right. It needs more."

"She likes the over-sized closet you added."

"Juanita picked out the turquoise to paint the dresser and headboard. She made use of much of the furniture we had stored here. Mom doesn't mind combining the housekeeping stores in the downstairs area. After all, she has the elevator." Jemma adjusted the step stool and looked up at the beadboard ceiling. "Is this where you want it?"

"Si. She talked about it being too dark on this side of the room." Miguel opened the box and removed the solar tube.

Jemma read the directions and cut a circular hole in the ceiling with the jigsaw. Miguel had checked the attic space earlier to be sure it was clear of wires and insulation. Miguel took the tube and returned to the top of the stairs and pulled down the folding steps for attic access. Jemma followed him up and went out a vent opening to walk on the roof. Her dad had insisted the oversized opening was hinged to make easy access for maintenance. With the rubber flange looped over her wrist and the dome in one hand, she rested a moment to look over at her cabin in the woods while Miguel drilled a hole in the roof to mark the center of the tube.

The trail ride to Racoon Run that afternoon had gone well but the overheard comment by one of the guests had stirred her CSI urges. "A simple murder. How hard could it be?" made her smile at the moment. She'd tell it to Tucker that night during their regular "good night" phone call and he'd again caution her about investigating on her own.

Miguel called to her so she removed some shingles, cut the circular hole in the roof, slid the uphill side of the flange under a shingle and nailed the downhill side to the roof. She sealed the flange, replaced some shingles and attached the dome. Jemma and Miguel returned to the interior room where Jemma secured the flange to the ceiling. Miguel folded up the drop cloth, careful to keep all the debris tucked in and grabbed the step stool. Jemma collected her tools and they both paused at the door to survey their handy work. Jemma looked closely at a vase on the dresser.

"Rooster feathers," Miguel said.

Jemma's immediate thought was of tickling Tucker with one, he'd grab it from her, then—

"From my first cock fight in Mexico." Miguel nodded to Jemma. "I understand. None of that allowed in the US."

Miguel's gift to Juanita of natural light was ready.

Chapter 8: Tuesday Evening

Death had greeted Jemma every day for the last few weeks. The kitties had grown into cats. Mice with their high pitched squeaks ran in the cabin, hid, then squeaked again. Eventually, the kitties played them to death and brought her the trophies. She loved the hunters but hated some of their instincts.

Aunt Alma fed the birds each day and JK and DT had graduated to catching birds in flight. Mice and moles were bad enough but birds were worse. Should they stop feeding the birds and affect the many? Was the sacrifice of the few worth it? Jemma opened the door and flung the dead bird out in the woods, then vacuumed and cleaned up the feathers before supper.

At the supper table, Juanita gushed about the natural light Miguel had given her room. "I had no idea such a thing was possible. Cutting through the ceiling and the roof, then using mirrors to send me day light. I will take pictures to send home to my parents. Thank you Miguel and Jemma."

Miguel simply nodded, but his smile showed his pleasure.

"It was Miguel's idea. Glad you like it." Jemma stared over Juanita's shoulder, blinked then looked again.

Juanita and the others turned to look but saw nothing out of the ordinary. "What did you see?"

"Nothing, really." Jemma cleared her throat to divert attention but everyone looked at her expectantly. "I though I saw Scott. Silly of me. He's been on my mind lately."

Juanita and Miguel crossed themselves then Juanita grabbed Miguel's hand.

"Maybe he didn't cross over yet," Bo said. "He could be waiting for Jemma to find out who wanted him out of the way. Didn't you say the club program was about photographing ghosts?"

"Bo, stop it. You're frightening us." Alma looked at Juanita, then Miguel. "He's talking nonsense."

"Scott could have found out that the ghost photographer had faked the photos. I know he was about to reveal something to the club, so maybe the ghost man had to stop him." Bo scanned the room as if hoping to see signs of a ghost.

"We have lots of ghost tales in these mountains." Lyle threw some salt over his shoulder, claiming to have spilled some earlier. "There's the one at the Horn in the West outdoor drama. A man's voice calls to actors who perform there."

His wife Pearle leaned in, her white hair shimmering in the light. "How about the one at the church in Valle Crucis where a preacher hung himself? The grooves are still in the ceiling joist."

"That's the story that Nicholson fellow lifted for that book *The Red Church*, isn't it?" Alma asked.

Lyle nodded to her. "There's another one from the old railroad depot in Todd where windows slam by themselves and the three footsteps fade to silence."

"Didn't the old Green Park Inn in Blowing Rock have a 'ghost register' at the front desk for visitors to record their experiences?" Pearle looked around the table as if expecting someone to verify her story.

"If ya'll don't quit, I'll be haunted by all the birds, moles and mice my kitties have recently killed. Pass me some of those potatoes, please. Let's talk about something else." Jemma reached out her hand and effectively stopped the ghost talk.

Alma rose to refill the bowls at the tables and made the announcement about the next day's activities. "At nine the riders leave for the ridge above Racoon Run and leave again at two for a ride to Rhymer Hill. Non-riders meet after breakfast for a bike ride on the Blue Ridge Parkway. Tomorrow evening, we'll cook steaks out by the corral and sing along with our own Bo and his guitar."

After supper, Juanita knocked on Jemma's cabin door. "Sorry to bother you but I was hoping you could help me."

"Come on in. I'll be glad to help." Jemma motioned her in, curiosity immediately aroused.

Juanita kept her eyes lowered and spoke quietly. "This is secret. No one must know." She raised her chin to look directly at Jemma.

"Of course." Juanita's face was within a foot of Jemma's so she stepped back. 'What is it?"

Juanita gave Jemma a quizzical look and stepped forward.

"There's no one else here. You don't have to whisper." Jemma leaned back.

"I am not whispering. Forgive me, but don't you like

me?" Juanita fingered the tiny cross on a delicate chain around her neck.

Bewildered, Jemma blurted, 'I think you're fine. Why?"

"You move away from me. You don't let me stand close."

Jemma paused. "Where are you comfortable when you talk to someone?"

"Here." She stepped in to about eighteen inches from Jemma.

"American's like more space. This is the right distance." Jemma stood three feet away and gestured the distance between them.

Juanita's eyes flashed understanding. "I thought you were cold to me. Is your culture, no?"

"Is my culture, yes." Jemma smiled to reflect her gentle teasing. "We keep further apart. I have another question. Do men from Mexico look directly at other people?"

Juanita nodded. "To men, yes. Not to women, at least not while in Mexico. It shows respect. Sometimes Miguel looks at women's eyes, but he explained that was the American way. It is confusing."

"It is, yes. If something else like this comes up, ask me or Alma. We want you to like it here."

She stuck out her chin, again. "I want to hire you to follow Miguel. I think he is seeing another woman." Her voice weakened. "I am so ashamed."

"Why? Why do you think that?" Jemma asked. Miguel had worked so hard to bring Juanita to the States. Juanita's fears had to be simple jitters about her new life.

"I am here only two weeks and he is going out tonight and does not tell me why or where. He tells me it is not a woman, but I do not know. Will you follow him?"

"Whoa there. First of all, I don't get paid and I wouldn't take money from you anyway. Second, what would you do if he was seeing someone?"

"I will fight for him. He is my man. I must know. Also this is a new country for me and I would get lost on the roads. You know the area. You must hurry. He leaves in a few minutes. Please help me. This is very important to me. He borrowed a truck from one of the wranglers." Juanita stepped toward the door.

"It's against my better judgment but I'll help you. Would you feed the cats?"

Jemma put on a dark baseball cap and lightweight jacket, tucking her braid under the jacket. In the dark, at six feet, she'd pass for a man with her loose-fitting dark jeans and riding boots. She hadn't had time to change after leading the afternoon trail ride.

Jemma left the truck lights off and gave Miguel a long lead all the way to Elk Creek Road. When he took a left, she followed then turned on her lights. At that point, she figured he wouldn't suspect that he was being followed. After a mile, he turned left past a feeder creek and wound back into the hills. Jemma slowed when she saw dozens of trucks and a few cars parked on both sides of the gravel road. Miguel wasn't visiting a woman.

She parked, thankful for the cloud cover that made it a moonless night. She made her way along the outside of the vehicles just as two men returned to their trucks. "Better luck next time," she heard one say.

She picked up her pace toward a lighted area near an old barn. Roosters crowed. Men cheered as if watching a sporting event. She dared not get close but saw feathers flying when one man left a space in the ring of spectators.

She gasped and turned back to her truck. That sickening glimpse had been enough. Miguel would have some explaining to do tomorrow. As she approached her truck, she ducked as a dozen or so men walked the road on the other side.

"Bet some of those photographs are beauties," one voice said.

"Too bad my cock lost."

Jemma recognized the voice and chanced a look through the cab as the gamblers passed her passenger door. It was the judge.

***

Tucker's face felt raw after his second shave of the day. Why had he agreed to this? He should have declined. A new case, Jemma, suspects to investigate. But the past had come to the present and he had to figure out if Wanda still had the power to invade his life, to take over his thoughts.

He met Wanda in the lobby of Fairfield Inn and Suites and took her to The Best Cellar in nearby Blowing Rock. She had on a summer dress and heels. He was glad he'd put on a sport coat and tie and looked like he belonged with her. When she snuck a shrimp off his appetizer plate, he caught her hand and led the fork to her mouth where she slipped it between her lips.

"Your turn," she said, and fed him from her plate. The waiter watched her and sent him a knowing smile that said, "Way to go, dude."

Tucker swore every man in the restaurant looked her over more than once. He slid the vase of flowers to one side so he could see her better. When she leaned forward, her hair fell in a half moon around her face.

"Remember swimming at the Granny Hole?" she asked, her voice almost a purr.

"It was filled in for a few years. Too much trash left from beer parties." A flitter of a thought of Jemma crossed his mind. The Granny Hole was only five miles below the ranch.

Wanda whispered, "I accidentally left my panties there after one of our visits."

Tucker's heart thudded when she leaned back and sipped her wine. "What about our walks around Price Lake?" he asked softly.

"If the Parkway Rangers had patrolled the trail at the right time, you would have an 'indecent exposure' arrest on your record." She licked a drop of wine from her lip.

Hours slipped by before Tucker noticed the last of the other guests leaving. "We'd better go. I have an early appointment tomorrow." When he put his napkin on the table and stood, he almost knocked over the flowers. Suspect Leslie Fine gardened and handled flowers. How did that fit with Scott? Despite his wonderful dinner and Wanda at his side, his thoughts shifted to the case while he drove back to Boone.

"Won't you come up?" Wanda asked in the hotel parking lot after he opened the passenger door.

He shook his head. "I'm not ready for that."

"Oh? That's too bad. Well, I'm not leaving for a few days. You have more time." She pulled him to her, kissed him thoroughly, then waved goodbye before going inside.

The message machine blinked red when he got home. Jemma had left four messages. The last one was to call her, no matter what time he got in. First he changed and slipped into bed, his body still humming from the evening but his thoughts elsewhere.

"Sorry it's so late. What's this about the judge?"

Jemma told him about the cockfight and he snapped into alert mode and grabbed the note pad from the bedside table. "Do you know when the next fight is scheduled?"

"No, but I may be able to find out."

"I thought you said you 'happened upon' this. Is there something you're not telling me?"

She hesitated a beat too long. "I simply followed a line of pickup trucks down on Elk Creek Road. Bo may be able to find out about the next one. You know how he hears things."

"You weren't following up on Scott's murder?"

She spoke quickly, too quickly. "No, not at all. You asked me not to. Were you able to find out anything about Tammy?"

"You were right about her. Thanks."

"Ah, hah. Alma told me to help you and to stay in the background. She said to let you have the glory and take the risks."

Tucker didn't quite believe her. "I don't know about the glory, but the entire sheriff's department will ferret out the full story. Once everything is finished, including the trial and sentencing, I'll let you know a little more. I can't afford to let out any information until the end. I do appreciate your help."

"You can show me your appreciation this weekend. I miss you."

Her voice deepened and invited Tucker to play. The timing wasn't right for the truth but when would it be? Instead, he took a deep breath and was about to speak.

"What is it? You can tell me."

The truth, he had to tell her. "Wanda, an old friend, is in town this week on business and we want to get together this weekend. She owns a chain of pet stores and a franchisee wants to open a branch here." Moments passed while Tucker gauged her reaction … anger, disappointment, jealousy?

"Invite her down to the ranch. I'd love to meet her and find out some of your exploits."

That was unexpected. "Uh, I'm not sure."

"Is she an old girlfriend? You said you'd never had a serious relationship before me."

"That isn't entirely true." Tucker sat up in bed.

"You lied to me? I thought you valued complete honesty above all. Did you kiss her? Recently?"

Her voice rose an octave. How did she know?

"Yes, she caught me by surprise Monday night."

"I see. No wonder you didn't call last night."

Tucker paused. "I want to be honest with you. She'll be leaving after this weekend and that'll be the end of it."

"You want to be honest. Answer this. Is that all I mean to you? What about being true?"

"Jemma, don't be like that," Tucker said into the dial tone.

***

Jemma hung up the phone and lay back against the pillows, gathering Jemma Kitty close to her. Too stunned to cry or even think, she stared at JK's shiny grey coat, petting her with long, calm strokes. "I don't believe this is happening to me," she said to the cat. "He kissed someone else. Not only that, he was in love before and he lied about it. He gave my kisses to someone else."

She should be calm about this. Withdraw. Protect herself. He betrayed her. She may have felt they belonged together but he didn't. It was another one-sided thing where she assumed depth that wasn't there. She slipped the sheet over her head and curled up on her side. Only then did she let tears fall freely and sobbed into JK's warm body. JK purred loudly then left. Too close for comfort.

Jemma went to the bathroom and used toilet tissue to dry her tears and blow her nose.

Juanita was willing to fight for her man. The difference was, Juanita was worth it and Miguel loved her. He'd talked about her for months and arranged for her to move here. They had wedding plans.

Jemma, on the other hand, had no career, held low income jobs, had no sense of style and was too tall. Her hips were spread from so many hours in the saddle. Callouses upon callouses lined her fingers from working with horses, hammers and wood. None of her clothes were trendy or even unstained.

Her single braid hadn't been cut in a decade and had never been in style. What did she have to offer a man? No wonder Tucker had lost interest. What does a woman do when being herself had degenerated into no self-interest?

Chapter 9: Wednesday Morning

"**Heard** you were with some looker besides Jemma on Monday night," Graves said when Tucker met him on the way to the chief's office Wednesday morning.

"How did you know about that?"

"Sit in the front window of a two-story Mindy's and you get noticed. Does Jemma know about it?"

"I told her late last night. She didn't say much."

"I don't expect she did. When it comes to the heart, she'd rather withdraw and lick her wounds. My wife would give me the silent treatment for days. I gather you told her after she told you about the judge." Graves shook his head. "That'll be the last time she tells you anything."

"You know me, blunt and honest." Why did he feel like he'd broken some code of behavior?

"Sometimes that works. Other times, you have to pick the moment and how you tell a woman."

They entered the chief's office and stood before her desk.

"What do you have?"

Tucker told her about the judge and cockfighting.

"Good work. See if you can find out when the next fight is. Who's your contact?"

"Jemma Chase. Now hold on," he rushed to add. "She happened upon it near her valley, a few miles from Blue Falls Ranch."

"She tipped you off about the nurse's penchant for horse doping, too. I meant what I said about keeping her off this case."

"I told her." Weak, even to his own ears.

"Do I need to make it clear to her?"

"No, ma'am. I'll handle it. We're headed to Tammy's house with a warrant to search for the missing trophy, the laptop and signs relating to horse medicine. The judge is due here around eleven to sign his statement."

"I'll be watching that interview. Keep it on Scott and don't tip him off on the cockfighting. Tap anyone you need to plan the gambling bust."

Tucker and Graves spent the next hour recruiting help from the Boone Police for the gambling ring roundup. Everyone was eager to be involved in stopping the cockfights. When the alert went out, everyone would have to react immediately and as silently as possible.

Tucker and Graves drove to Tammy's house between Boone and Blowing Rock. The small frame house, probably built in the 1980s, sat back off a gravel road. The door knocker was an upside down horse shoe. It didn't seem to bring her luck. Tammy answered.

She looked at the warrant, grabbed her bag and headed to her car. "This is ridiculous. I'm late for work. Lock up when you're finished."

After she left, Graves said, "Wonder what she had in the car or in that big purse. A mini-laptop wouldn't be hard to hide."

"The warrant only lets us check the house." The furniture was beige but the decorations were horse related—curtains, pillows, throw rugs. Framed photographs of horses were clustered on the wall above the sofa. Above a corner table, dozens of ribbons lined the walls. A round doily centered on the table reserved a space for something large. Must be for the trophy she expected to win. The place was neat, clean and impersonal except for the horses. No photos of people. The laptop was not found but Scott's photography trophy was hidden in her underwear drawer. Tucker photographed the drawer and bagged the trophy as evidence. A thorough search of the kitchen and bathroom showed no poisons other than regular household cleaners. Her access to drugs at the doctor's office could explain the absence at the house.

Her bank book, however, showed a one thousand dollar check made out last month to Scott. Her balance wasn't high, but neither was her income. Tucker opened the door to the spare bedroom which doubled as storage space. After photographing the room, he checked some of the moving boxes that were taped shut. Unlike the rest of the house, dust flew when he opened one which was full of dishes. He figured these were from her move four years ago. Under the spare bed he found a suitcase. From the scrape marks in the dust, it had been put there recently. The suitcase held folded clothes and maps of Texas. Her passport was current. "Graves," he called. He showed him the suitcase.

"We should have enough here to question her further," Graves said.

"She could keep this packed for vacations. The other items in this room have been here a long time."

"Face it, we need to talk to her again and this would clinch it. Aren't you scheduled to interview the judge soon?"

Tucker photographed everything in the suitcase and put it back in place. He wasn't sure Tammy was about to flee.

"This'll put you back in the lead, ahead of Jemma," Graves marked the bank book as evidence.

Tucker froze, stifling the defensive remark he was about to make. Grave's simple words struck a raw nerve. He envied Jemma's knack for stumbling onto clues.

Graves looked at Tucker and shrugged. "It's the truth, like it or not. Some of the guys are betting on the girl. What we found here isn't much to go on but it is evidence."

"The truth," his personal mantra, didn't sit well with him this time. He locked the door when they left the house, aware of a tightness in his jaw which didn't go away even when he turned in the evidence and met the judge in the interview room.

***

Jemma surprised Bo and asked him to lead the morning trail ride to the Ridge above Racoon Run while she slipped to the back of the line of horses and riders to be with Miguel. She decided to be blunt because she couldn't figure out a way to ask the question with finesse. That's her. Blunt, masculine, uneducated, lowly-jobbed and uninspired. No wonder Tucker was attracted to someone else.

"You did know that cockfighting is illegal in this country?"

"This I did hear." Miguel tightened on the reins to slow his horse to match Jemma's pace. "So I did not tell Juanita that I am going to such an event."

"She was really worried about you, you know … about where you were going."

"She should not have been." Miguel's eyes narrowed. "For when I came there, many Americans—rich men they looked to be—were there as well. Someone said one of them was from the law, but he cheered like the rest, and even took pictures."

The judge, Jemma thought. Did he think no one would know him.

"So I think I have worried Juanita for nothing."

"Oh, it's illegal all right," Jemma said. "It's inhumane to treat animals like that."

"Americanos have strange ideas about animals. They eat pigs, cows and chickens but not roosters or dogs. They put chickens in tight sheds with no air, make them lay eggs, then slaughter them. But it is illegal to watch them fight, using their natural instincts."

Brandy tried to get ahead of Miguel's horse. Jemma reined her in and patted her on the neck to calm her. "That's right. Every country has laws it thinks are important. We don't like cockfighting. You don't seem surprised that I brought up this subject."

"I saw you last night. I thought you enjoyed the sport."

Jemma almost gagged at the thought. "No. I was there for other reasons."

He stopped his horse and Jemma did the same. "Are you investigating someone? I heard that you catch criminals. I am not a criminal. I am here legally and do not break laws." He looked away. "I do not break important laws."

"This could be an important law if you are caught breaking it. You need to promise never to go to one of those cock fights again. And, I want you to tell me when and where the next one is."

Miguel shook his head. "I don't want to get my friends in trouble."

"Right now, I'm trying to keep you and your friends out of trouble. When is the next event?"

"I don't know. This was my first one in this country. I'll have to ask my friend."

Jemma nodded then clicked and Brandy trotted along side one of the guests. Jemma chatted and moved up to another, answering a question or two about the horse. She moved up to the middle of the train of horses and stayed, letting Bo enjoy his spot at the head of the line. Brandy settled into a walk and Jemma inhaled the warm, moist summer air. Queen Anne's lace stood tall beside the trail with its spot of red in the middle of the lace flower. The big leaves of mayapple hugged the ground in the woods. The apple wouldn't be ripe enough for the animals to eat until fall. The roots and leaves were poisonous all the time. Wonder if that could have been used to kill Scott? Mayapple was plentiful in the Appalachian woods. Once back to the barn, she helped the guests dismount then instructed them about lunch in the dining room. She tended to Brandy, taking off the saddle even though she'd have to put it back on by two for the afternoon ride. All the while, her mind was on Tucker.

Jemma eased into the kitchen through the back screen door. Juanita rushed to her, moved to hug her, then hesitated.

Jemma opened her arms. "Hugs are okay."

Juanita squeezed her tight and gushed "thank you" two or three times.

Jemma recalled that morning at breakfast, she had sat next to Juanita and whispered, "You don't have to worry about another woman. You need to be direct and ask Miguel about last night." Feeling good about helping Juanita, she helped carry out the last serving platter.

At noon, Jemma sat across from Juanita who nodded and looked shyly at Miguel. Another mystery solved by famous CSI wannabe Jemma Chase, she thought ruefully.

"Name your poison." Bo pointed to the serving bowls.

"That's not funny and you know it." Jemma grabbed the closest bowl and served herself.

"I'd take foxglove." Randy spooned some refried beans onto his plate and handed the bowl to Alma with a wink. "It grows around here and overloads the heart. It's the source of digitalis."

"Give me horse chestnut. I think those nuts are so pretty." Pearle's smile held a hint of secret information.

She always looks so put together, Jemma thought. Her white hair shimmered, her makeup made her look sophisticated. Even though they had retired to the valley decades ago, their frequent meals at the ranch made her and Lyle seem like family.

"Jimsonweed seeds are tough on horses," Miguel said.

Jemma marveled at Miguel's openness since Juanita had joined the ranch. His gregarious nature was outed.

"Water hemlock will kill a cow," Lyle said, then stroked his short gray beard.

"In the fall, doll's eyes—some call it white baneberry— with those tall dark red stalks would do the job." Alma passed a plate. "For that matter, Yew bark and leaves and any part of ivy are toxic."

"Ivy? Are you talking about mountain laurel?" Pearle asked.

Alma nodded.

"How would you fix something like that?" Lyle asked.

Juanita's eyes widened. "These tamales?"

"No. Poison. Take foxglove, for example."

"Should I be worried?" Pearle squeezed her husband's hand. Lyle's bewildered look made everyone laugh.

Jemma gave up hoping the conversation would turn to another topic.

"You could boil it into a tea," Alma suggested.

Jemma joined in. "Would that destroy the poison?"

"I don't know. Maybe if you let the sun steep it for a day. Some does tea like that." Alma looked to Pearle for confirmation.

"What about roots and such?" Lyle couldn't let the subject lay.

Juanita fingered the cross on the chain around her neck. "You would dry it, then mash it with mortar and pestle. Grind it down, like corn into corn meal."

Bo slapped Miguel on the back. "You better not cross that one. She has a backup plan."

"No, no." Juanita grabbed Miguel's hand. "Is not true."

"He is teasing you," Miguel said in English.

Alma stood and announced to everyone. "We wish to congratulate our neighbors here. Sugar Mountain dedicated the ski patrol building at the top of the mountain to them. It's the Pearle and Lyle Bishop Summit House. How many of us will ever have a building named after us?"

Jemma joined the impromptu toast to the couple who'd been ski patrollers for a quarter of a century.

After dinner, Jemma stopped Bo. "Would you lead

the ride this afternoon? I have something I need to do."

"Following up on Scott?"

"Something like that."

"Go for it. Miguel and I will do dastardly deeds on the ride without you."

Jemma gathered some photos and put them in the largest handbag she had. It was over a decade old but the stitching still held the leather together. She drove the pickup to the Watauga Democrat office in the Industrial Park on the east side of Boone and waited in line at the counter.

Jemma introduced herself to the desk clerk after she had handled the two people in line ahead of her. She leaned in and lowered her voice. "I'm sorry about Scott. Not to be untimely, but I loaned him some of my photos and I need them back. They're easy to spot—they're of horses."

The clerk looked at the three people who just came in, looked around for help, then said, "His desk is in the third room on the right. I shouldn't do this, so make it quick."

Jemma thanked her and headed to the desk. She figured the detectives had already been there but she wanted to see for herself. She looked through folders, stacks of photographs, drawers, on scratch pads, glancing around every few moments but no one took an interest in her. Emboldened, she felt for secret compartments on the desk, false bottoms in the drawers, even turned the chair upside down. One of the folders must have held pictures of photography club members. The detectives took everything. Jemma gave up and left, flashing a photo from her bag to the clerk as justification for the search.

Undeterred, Jemma drove to Appalachian State University in downtown Boone and waited for Summer in her campus office. The walls held photos of athletic women, some posed in uniform, some caught in motion during competition and training, and a few tasteful candid shots in the locker room. At least seventy-five shots hung on the walls and a dozen frames were propped in a corner on the floor.

"I started collecting those when I first took this job a few years back," Summer said by way of greeting Jemma.

Jemma pointed to a group of track team members at the finish line. "Perfect subjects, fit women in action."

"Women's muscles delineate differently from men. See these triceps?" Summer traced the form on the photograph. "They are rounder, more subtle."

"I see what you mean. Wish I was in as good shape at these women."

"You probably are, under all those old clothes. Riding firms the arms and back, not to mention the calves. Bet I could show you in a good light if you want me to photograph you." Summer felt Jemma's upper arm.

Summer's grip was firm but seductive; it lingered a bit too long.

"I can see it now. Me standing next to my horse in a bikini and riding boots." Jemma walked to a different wall of photos to get out of arms' reach of Summer.

"We could put you in stretchable fabric to show your form but not expose your skin."

"Whoa there. I'll have to think about this." Jemma's old self-image of being too tall and ordinary rose and threatened to blot out the real reason for the visit.

"You know, you could be a stunning woman if you made a little effort. Your horse tail braid is a couple of feet too long, your eyebrows need work. It's like you try to cover up your female side. My athletes are both strong and feminine." Summer pointed to two of the pictures on the wall, then pinned Jemma with a direct look.

Jemma broke the eye contact, tapped her bag then fumbled opening it. "I appreciate the compliment. I stopped by to give you a copy of the photograph I promised at last month's meeting. In all the upheaval with Scott, I forgot to hand them out." She handed Summer the photo, careful not to touch fingertips. "How well did you know Scott?"

Summer smiled at Jemma, as if she knew a subject change when presented one, and rounded her desk and sat in the chair. "We're both local so I've known him all my life." Her eyes clouded; she took a deep breath. "Our families go to the same church. He started at the newspaper as a photographer but wanted to do more investigative reporting. He talked about it all the time at Murphy's. His advice improved my photography immensely, as you can see." She nodded toward the wall of photographs. Sadness replaced her flirty demeanor.

"Any ideas on who would want to poison Scott?"

She shook her head. "He was harmless and a fun guy. I guess it was someone who thought he knew something. The last time I really talked with him, he had a lead on that big story he was always hoping for."

Jemma frowned, wondering if that were true. "Will you be at Aaron's tomorrow night?"

"I suppose so. He's excited about showing his pictures in the same house as the ghost." Summer held up the gift. "Thank you for the photo."

Jemma left the office, knowing she'd learned something about Summer but not quite sure what it was. She hesitated, then borrowed a phone at the reception desk.

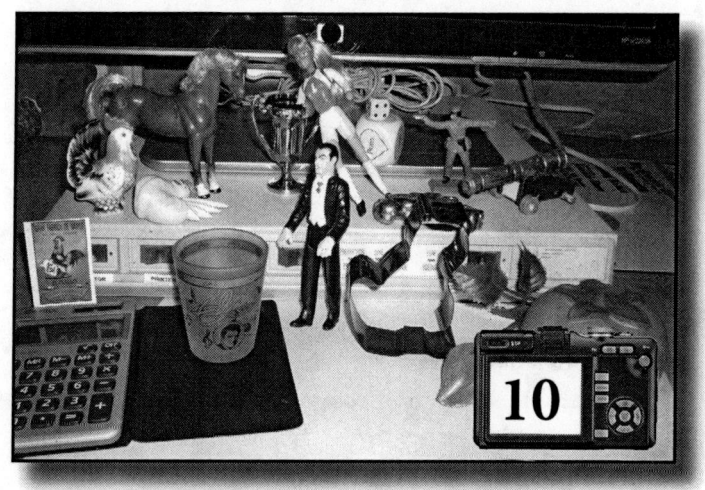

Chapter 10: Wednesday Afternoon

Back at the sheriff's complex, Tucker snatched a moment to load the photos of Tammy's house on his computer before meeting the judge in the hall.

As he followed Tucker down the hall, the judge said, "Don't let me forget to say a few words to the chief while I'm here. She's good at keeping you boys in line."

Tucker smiled appropriately when they sat in one of the investigation rooms. "I thought you might appreciate the quiet to read over your statement."

The judge read the statement and signed it. "Tragedy about Scott. Any progress on the investigation?"

"You know we can't divulge anything about it." Tucker tamped down the sudden image of Scott dead on the game room floor.

"The police and their secrets. Until trial, that is."

"You've heard all kinds of motives during your years at court." Tucker relaxed in his seat to signal the judge that this was just routine.

"Sometimes I think certain secrets deserve to remain

private. Don't get me wrong, I believe in and uphold the law. Mitigating circumstances make my job tough at times." The judge mirrored Tucker's move. "Spouse abuse, endangering a minor, an old murder. I don't agree with murder but I can understand the reasons behind some of them. Frustration drives people to do desperate acts. Sex, wives running around, blackmail. I've been at court a long time." The judge pinched the bridge of his nose and briefly closed his eyes.

"I always heard that secrets were like a butterfly near the highway, fluttering through life until flattened by the past."

The judge nodded sagely in agreement.

The move was touching but theatrical. "Motives acted out. They're always a combination of the seven deadly sins and the ten commandments. My job is to find those who let their lives cross society's boundaries. Your job is to punish those we catch."

"Provide a fair trial, you mean. If a law is broken, then I punish them."

"Sometimes I think my job's easier than yours. Mine's figuring out what happened and bringing in the culprit. Yours is more soul-searching; you make them pay. You'd have to lead an exemplary life to be able to live with yourself." Tucker smiled just a bit, wanting to softly rattle the smug man, all the while aware the chief watched through the two-way mirror. "When murder is involved, I have to use those reasons to find the killer. I find out the little vices of suspects and follow the trails to possible motives. We all have secrets. Don't you?" Tucker let his voice harden on the question.

The judge smirked. "Am I a suspect? Not likely. You know how much my reputation means to me. I would never do anything to jeopardize my standing in our fine community." He stood to signal control in ending the interview right before the door opened and the chief walked in.

"Are you finished here?" she asked Tucker.

"Yes. Thank you, Judge, for coming in." Tucker followed them out, aware that the chief had stepped in to stop the interview. Reputation topped the judge's list of motivation.

"Hello Detective, are you ready for me?" Leslie asked in a soft voice when Tucker passed the line of framed photographs of former Watauga County Sheriffs. She pointed to one with a cowboy hat. "Is he related to you? You have a similar look around the eyes."

"Distant cousin." Tucker watched the judge and chief leave together and took Leslie's arm a little too abruptly, causing her to lose balance. "Are you okay? I didn't mean to do that. Let's go to the interview room and sit you down before I do any more damage."

"Lead the way. I'm more stable than you think." Leslie followed Tucker but caught her breath when he opened the interrogation room door. "Oh, my. This room is so ... sterile."

"Yes, ma'am, I suppose it is."

She sat and read the statement as soon as he passed it over.

Tucker worked to focus on Leslie's fingers while she signed her name in an effort to get his mind off the judge and the silent rebuff his boss had given him. He wouldn't have brought up the cockfighting. Was the chief being extra cautious because Tucker had used Jemma's information?

"Is that all?" Leslie paused after opening her purse to

put away her reading glasses.

Tucker glimpsed a rosary. Not that many Catholics lived in the mountains. He'd mistakenly pegged her as local. Now he focused. "Almost. What do you know about Scott's mini laptop?"

Leslie frowned in concentration. "It was a pretty color. I'm afraid all I know about computers relates to email and photography software. Everything else is scrambled eggs." Leslie shifted and folded her trembling hands on top of her purse.

"Do you have children?"

Her tight smile softened. "Three, grown and on their own. My husband and I are proud of all of them."

Fear was normal in these situations. Most people never even saw the inside of a sheriff's complex. "Did they go to school with Scott?"

"I suppose so. He wasn't a part of their crowd. My children were serious about studies." Leslie sat up even taller. "Two graduated from ASU. The third, my youngest son, is going into the priesthood."

"Reminds me of my cousin. She adored raising children and is proud of her kids. Still, she misses them and the purpose they gave to her life. Know what I mean?"

"I do. They're busy with jobs and new friends." She glanced down at her hands and adjusted her engagement ring so the diamond sat top and center. "I spend time now with my husband, my garden and my church. What does your cousin do now?"

"She's a First Responder. Her husband's Catholic, like you. My cousin converted to marry him. She likes the confession part; says it's cheaper than therapy. You've probably met them since there's only one Catholic Church in the area." Tucker mentioned their names and

Leslie said she'd seen them at church. Leslie had stiffened when he'd mentioned confession. "His parents were more Orthodox when they moved here in the seventies but they've adapted to this church. No threat of ex-communication for marrying someone not born Catholic. How about you?"

Leslie paused then gave him a tight smile. "I'm happy with this church."

Tucker thanked her for coming, stood and walked Leslie to the front door. "Your visit with Scott last month, what was that about?"

She blinked twice. "He wanted help choosing entries for the Grandfather contest. He asked a number of us and took a census. It must have worked because he won."

"And celebrated with one shot too many."

She frowned. "Will I be hearing from you again?"

"Only if you contact me with information. We appreciate your cooperation."

Tucker returned to his desk; he and Graves compared notes. "Where did Tammy work before she moved here?"

"Winston-Salem, one of the assisted living homes."

Tucker searched through a desk drawer and found a business card. "I met one of their detectives at a training session last year."

When the detective answered, he said that he remembered Tucker.

"We have a case here involving a nurse and poisoning. She used to work in Winston." Tucker gave the dates and details. "Do you recall any cases, maybe unexpected deaths, that occurred around four years ago?"

"We did have a series of three about that time. Nothing was ever proven. Let me check the name."

Tucker held on for a few moments.

Another detective walked up. "Have you heard from Jemma today? Maybe she knows something about Tammy." He put a toy horse on the desk, grinned and left.

"I'd say your money's on Jemma," Tucker said, without even looking at the man. "This office is too small," he grumbled to Graves.

His contact returned to the line. "Did you say Tammy Portsmith? She was one of the two nurses we suspected but couldn't find a motive for either of them. No money or inheritance was involved. I'll send you a copy of what we have."

After he hung up the phone, Tucker threw down his pen. "More circumstantial evidence. These are pin pricks but not enough to pop her balloon." Tucker grabbed his things and turned to Graves. "I'll be at the gun club if anyone needs me."

"Practicing for our 'shoot don't shoot' night? You like that practice combat course with no lights or flashlights, don't you? Besides, you have a record to protect, no good guys shot by mistake." Graves shut down his computer and prepared to leave also.

Tucker shook his head. "Time to shoot off some steam."

Chapter 11: Wednesday Afternoon

Jemma gripped the steering wheel as she wound along Castle Ford Road toward the gun club, not because of the numerous curves—this was comparatively flatter than many mountain roads—but because she felt like a failure in giving in to a compulsion to see Tucker.

She tucked a stray lock of hair behind her ear, made a left, then a right onto a pot-holed gravel drive, drove slowly between a cattail filled bog on one side and a creek on the other and past an open metal gate. She parked in front of a tan cement block building with three shooting areas to her left. Each area's roofs were trimmed in dark green and held up by hand-hewn logs, a job which she hoped she'd never have to do. She took a deep breath, looked around and expelled sharply when she spotted Tucker's vehicle. A barn swallow called from a tree near the creek.

Gunshots echoed in the wide valley. She found Tucker alone in the handgun shooting area located toward the entrance gate and held back until he stopped firing to check his score on the target.

When he removed his hearing protection, she walked

up behind him. "You've invited me many times to join you here." She wiped her palms on her jeans.

Tucker's head jerked around. His eyes told her she was the last person he wanted to see.

Jemma stepped back. "Sorry. I made a mistake. Pretend I never came." She turned to go, ready to run back to the truck.

"Jemma, you took me by surprise is all. Don't be so defensive."

Jemma sucked in her breath. "I'd like a lesson if you have the time."

Tucker looked at the target then back at Jemma. "Dues are a hundred and fifty a year, plus a fifty dollar initiation fee."

"Oh, I didn't think of that." Now what? "Could you walk me through it and not fire the gun? Dad trained me with a shotgun and a rifle so I'm not completely ignorant."

Tucker shook his head, then briefly smiled. "I reckon we can test the limits of the gun club rules. Come on over here."

Jemma felt like an eager puppy, but tightened up at Tucker's serious demeanor.

"A semi-automatic, like this one, has only one chamber, which is an integral part of the barrel. It has no cylinder, and therefore cannot be mistaken for a revolver." Tucker narrowed his eyes as if to check if Jemma understood.

He's upset, Jemma thought, noting the tightness around his eyes. If only she could massage his shoulders.

"In the revolver, cartridges are loaded into chambers in the cylinder. The most common number is six, but there are many variations, especially in smaller calibers.

The cylinder is rotated by the gun's mechanism so that the chambers revolve around a central axis, which brings the cartridges one by one into line with the barrel."

Jemma shifted her weight and struggled to keep from zoning out when he talked about a gun that wasn't even here.

"Instead, the cartridges are loaded into a metal magazine or clip." Tucker released the clip and handed it to her.

She looked it over and handed it back to him, happy that her fingers grazed his.

He quickly continued. "This clip is then inserted into the butt of the pistol like this. The clip contains a spring, which pushes the cartridges upward for feeding into the chamber. When the auto is fired, the force of the recoil is used to drive back the slide. As the slide flies backward, the empty cartridge case is extracted from the chamber and thrown out through the ejector port." He pointed to the port.

Jemma took the opportunity to touch the gun, anything to slow his rapid-fire lecture. Her ruse to see him backfired; he used the textbook information to keep her emotionally distant.

"The rearward force of the slide also cocks the hammer. Now the slide is slammed forward by the pressure of a powerful spring. As it moves forward, it picks up the top cartridge in the clip and pushes it into the chamber. Depending on the power of the weapon, it may also be locked into place by some mechanism. Once the slide stops moving, the pistol is ready to fire." He aimed the gun toward the target and imitated squeezing off a shot. "To save your hearing, I won't actually shoot."

"May I hold it?"

"Be careful. It doesn't have a safety."

She took the gun and held it in her right hand with her left supporting the butt. He rearranged her grip so her thumb was out of the way of the slide. All she could think about was the firmness of his touch when he adjusted her stance then looked over her shoulder at the firing range. The warmth of his body on this June day almost caused her to break out in sweat.

"Note that at this point the hammer is fully cocked; a simple pressure on the trigger will cause the pistol to go off. For this reason, most semi-automatics of older design do have safety catches of some sort. However, in recent years the trend has been toward auto pistols which do not cock themselves, but have to be fired double action, like a revolver."

Jemma sighted the target then flinched and pulled the trigger. Her hands jumped from the slight recoil. "Sorry, it was an accident," she blurted. Exactly the opposite of what she'd intended. She turned to face Tucker.

He reached for the gun and they bumped heads. His face turned red, he released the clip. "Don't you ever—"

"I didn't mean to. Sorry about the head thing, the ringing in the ears thing. This was a bad idea. I'm leaving now. See me walking away." Jemma had never before slunk, but she did this time. She stooped her shoulders, bent her knees and in general tried to get away without further damage.

***

Tucker slammed the front door to his house and headed to the shower. How did things get so complicated all of a sudden? The phone rang while his face was covered in soap suds and he had no choice but to let the answering machine record the call. Five minutes could make a difference in solving the case but finding the phone with soap in his eyes wasn't an option. Shower spray hit the tender spot on his head. If Jemma had called to apologize again, she could wait. He finished the shower and toweled off while checking the message.

"This is Wanda with a basket full of goodies hoping you're up for a picnic at the Blue Ridge Parkway overlook just north of Blowing Rock. I'll be there in half an hour in case you can join me. I'd hate to eat alone."

Same flirty attitude and short notice as years ago. Not what he had hoped for with the case but early evening with a beautiful woman would do just fine. Frustration left like morning mist. He took a moment to find a blue shirt to go with tan pants and loafers. He'd leave his badge and gun in the car. He felt downright light without a holster on his hip.

He parked next to her car at the overlook and went down into the trees to the left. The park rangers kept the view open so this secret spot was out of sight to visitors yet was still cleared of trees.

Wanda lay on a blanket with her eyes closed. "What couldn't you resist?" She sat up and watched him approach and sit beside her. "Me or the nourishment. Or could they be one and the same?"

"You are like a drink of sweet tea. Naughty and nice. Too much sugar could rot your teeth." He reached and gently removed a leaf from her shoulder. Her bright full skirt and white blouse with gathers at the neck made her look deceptively innocent.

She took his hand and brushed it over her cheek then kissed two of his fingers.

Tucker's world stood still as fire and ice filtered from his kissed fingers to the rest of him. His stomach growled.

She laughed softly and released him from the moment. "Why don't you open the wine? This white's from the Banner Elk Winery and I kept it chilled in a cooler in the car."

"How long have you planned this outing?"

"It came to me first thing this morning. I made a quick trip to the winery early this afternoon then stopped at Stick Boy Bakery for sandwiches. Cheese and crackers if you prefer."

Tiny hairs on the back of his neck prickled. Was it from the breeze or a feeling of being trapped in a velvet snare? He opened the wine, poured a glass for her and one for himself. He leaned back on his elbows and gazed off into the distance. He couldn't quite see the tall buildings of Charlotte, but the air was fairly clear with a hint of the blue haze of the mountains.

He took a sip of wine, planning to make the one glass last since he had to drive home. He took another drink, set his glass down on a flat rock and lay back on the blanket.

Wanda mimicked his move. "What do you see in that cloud?"

"A kitchen chair. What about you?"

"A horse. See, its tail is taking shape. Most cloud pictures turn into animals to me."

"You're in the pet business." Tucker closed his eyes for a moment, thinking of horses, drifting to Jemma's ranch then to Tammy's riding competition.

"Maybe wine wasn't such a good idea," Wanda said.

Tucker opened his eyes. "What do you mean?"

"Two sips and next thing I know you are snoozing."

"Was I out long?"

"Ten minutes. That's all I allowed my ex when he

dozed off in the daytime."

Great. He could now be compared to his old foe. Tucker sat up. "Didn't sleep well last night. Too much going on. It isn't you." He rubbed his face to clear his groggy mind.

"And here I thought our dinner last night had you so riled up you tossed and turned because you didn't come up to my hotel room." She paused but he didn't reply. "Have a sandwich, maybe that will wake you." Wanda handed him a wrapped one, unwrapped her own and tore off a piece.

Tucker took the sandwich and watched Wanda pop the bread into her mouth. Wide awake, he reminded himself to mind his manners. She was ready to play; the neck of her blouse drooped and her bare feet and legs were angled toward him seductively. But he already had a playmate. Not that he and Jemma had talked about keeping things exclusive.

Wanda sipped her wine. "This always was a favorite place of mine. I'm not in a hurry now. I have all evening."

Tucker finished his wine. The choice was his.

***

Normally, steak cookout night was one of Jemma's favorites. Alma rang the dinner bell and guests came from their cabins or the lodge to the stone fire pit area below the pond with a view into the pasture. Bo and Miguel wheeled out the gas-fired grill, a fifty-five gallon drum cut in half longways which Jemma and Bo had built last year. They also wheeled out a buffet line serving cart which housed cubby holes for plates, cups, eating utensils, condiments, a coffee urn, a cooler with ice for canned drinks and large jugs of water, sweet tea and lemonade. The bottom half of one side folded down for the serving table; the raised top half became an awning. Most guests sat on benches around the pond or next to the corral. A couple of picnic tables were used by folks who couldn't eat off their laps but most enjoyed the casual atmosphere of outdoor eating.

"Grab a plate and let my brother, tonight's cook, know how you like your steaks." Alma paused until the guests and hands quieted down. "Chicken and deer sausage is on there, too. Corn on the cob is on the end of the grill. Fill your plates from the sideboard with slaw, green beans, baked beans, beets, rolls and pickles. The pickled okra came from Todd General Store. The watermelon ones I made myself. Use cups for drinks and fill up. The jug on the end is unsweet tea."

A line quickly formed and guests chatted about the trail ride that day; some talked about the bike ride. Bo strummed his guitar a bit, tuning it then playing tunes intended as background music. That is, until the line died down and it was time for the help to fill their plates. Miguel and Juanita sat so close together Jemma couldn't see how they managed to eat. Part of the time, he fed her then she did likewise, accompanied by soft words Jemma couldn't hear.

One of the guests came up to Jemma while she grabbed a cup of iced tea. "I want to thank you for all you've done for us."

"What do you mean?" Jemma tried to think of something different that had happened on a ride but couldn't.

"This vacation is the best thing that's happened to us in two years. My wife survived chemo and chose a trip to Blue Falls Ranch to celebrate. I was skeptical but it's been a true escape and helped us put our lives back into perspective."

"I'm so glad things are going better for you. Hearing your story means a lot to me." Jemma watched when he returned to his wife. She raised her cup in salute. Maybe something as simple as helping someone enjoy a vacation could enrich lives and was a worthwhile endeavor.

Bo, Jemma, Alma and Randy found an empty bench and claimed it as their own. Bo peeled the shuck off his corn and bit into the ear, never minding the silk. "How'd you get that knot on your head?" he asked Jemma.

Jemma bought some time by completely chewing a piece of steak, hoping no one expected an answer.

"Well?"

"Gun club," she mumbled, acutely aware of the flush creeping up her neck. "I bumped into Tucker at the gun club this afternoon. He showed me a little about using a pistol, my hand bounced, I panicked and then, to top things off, I bumped heads with Tucker. There, are you satisfied?" Sometimes Jemma wished she didn't have such a close-knit family. Humiliations, bad moves, embarrassments had to be thoroughly inspected, even enjoyed, by everyone. This was no exception.

That led to a rehash of Monday's events when Bo surprised Jemma. "Tammy's a fine looking woman. Do you think she would go out with me?" He wiped the butter off his face with the back of his hand, saw Alma's horrified look, and quickly cleaned up with napkins.

"I don't know her that well, but she seems busy with working with a doctor and then training with her horse on weekends and evenings." Jemma tried not to think of the two of them together, like a Siamese cat and a Saint Bernard dog.

"She came on to me when we was walking around in the pasture taking pictures. It was like she was quizzin' me about horses, but I know underneath she was nervous about being attracted to me. Do you have her phone number?"

"The club president probably has it. I'll ask next time I see him." If she's guilty like I think she is, Jemma said to herself, you can visit her in jail.

"While you're at it," Alma said, "get Leslie's phone number. I want her recipe for keeping deer out of the garden. I'm tired of spraying that raw egg concoction after every rain."

"You could both try the phone book," Jemma snapped.

"It's not that urgent. I'll wait." Bo said and Alma nodded her agreement.

Many guests had finished with their meals. Apple pie and ice cream would be served later after the sing-a-long. "Listen up," Alma called out. "Meet at nine for tomorrow's trail ride to a secret location then again at two for the afternoon ride to Deer Springs. The van to Grandfather Mountain biosphere leaves at nine-thirty. Tomorrow evening, look forward to some square dancing. I'll leave out a box of full skirts for the ladies and leather vests for the gents after supper tomorrow. We'll clean up some of this while Bo plays his guitar."

Earlier Jemma had put a couple of wash tubs in the pasture just beyond the railing and had filled them with water. She handed a dozen apples to the guests and instructed them to put one apple at a time in the tubs. She whistled for Brandy who knew the drill well. Brandy and Visa and a couple of others trotted over and stuck their noses in the tubs. Bobbing for apples, ranch style, would keep the guests and horses entertained while Bo played and the hands cleaned up.

After supper, Jemma hung around in the ranch kitchen even though everything was put away.

"Why so glum?" Alma asked.

"Tucker's old girlfriend is back in town and he's seeing her this week." She explained the situation. "I don't know what to do."

"Leave it alone; she'll be gone after the weekend," Alma wrapped a lone piece of leftover pie and set it on the counter.

"What would you do, Juanita?"

"Show him what he's missing." Juanita looked at the top Jemma wore. "This looks like a man's shirt. No shape, no pattern. It hangs away from your middle."

"I have a hard time finding something to fit these long arms and legs. Will you help me? We can go through my closet and you can tell me what works." Jemma fiddled with her braid. "What about my hair?"

"I would have cut it long ago." Alma searched through papers in a drawer. "I have a friend, a cancer survivor, who used to cut hair. She'll do yours for free if you donate the hair to Locks of Love. Do you want me to call her?"

Whoa, too fast, Jemma thought, then looked at Juanita's shoulder length hair. Sometimes she wore it up and sometimes loose around her face, both worked with her face shape which Jemma thought was similar to her own. "I'll do it," Jemma announced before she could change her mind.

Alma phoned her friend. "She can do it now, if you want."

Jemma nodded, afraid to wait and think about it. "Juanita, want to go with me?"

Juanita looked to Alma who nodded her approval. The two discussed how short to cut it on the trip around the base of the mountain to Alma's friend. Juanita said that men like long hair but not too long; that it would make Jemma look more in style and younger. That did it, Jemma's qualms vanished. The travel and hair cut took less than an hour.

When they returned to the ranch, the two went directly to Jemma's wardrobe. Juanita dismissed most of the clothes but kept a few. They filled a large bag to donate to the thrift shop; the rest went into the trash. "I can add stitches here on this top to show off your waist. Don't you have a dress or a skirt?"

"No, I always wear pants, like Katherine Hepburn."

"Who?"

"Never mind. If Alma will let you off for lunch tomorrow, would you go to the thrift shop with me before the afternoon ride? Maybe you'll find something for yourself."

"I would like that. I have made a little money and would like some more clothes. Your Aunt Alma gave me these to work in. They fit but they're dull. Like your clothes."

Jemma fingered her relatively short hair. "I want to call him.

"Is too soon. Let him call you."

Jemma stared at herself for a long time in the mirror after Juanita left then checked Summer's websites. Photos of the college, women's sports, healthful living and enjoying today dominated the sites. Students had added their own photos.

Jazzed with energy over her hair cut, she looked around her remodeled first floor with a critical eye then went to her bedroom. No walls had been removed in the old cabin so the room was small with no closet. A wardrobe held her few remaining clothes. Restless, she grabbed her remodeling sketch and climbed the narrow stairs to the four small rooms and closet-sized half bath. At least the ceiling height had been oversized for the times and she didn't have to duck her head. If she knocked out the walls to three of the rooms and expanded the bath into the forth room, she could make a master suite. Since the half bath already existed, she wouldn't have to submit a septic permit. The two dormers in the front could be her sleeping section, the third bedroom could be a sitting space. Part of the forth would be a walk-in closet with built-in dressers and a full length mirror so she could see all six feet of herself at one time.

What about a soaker tub? Why not? And a separate tiled shower big enough not to need a curtain or glass door. She'd have to get a couple of strong exhaust fans to remove the moisture and keep mildew away.

She sighed and folded the sketch neatly in quarters, then stuck the corner in the space around a door frame. What good would all that luxury be if she didn't have Tucker to share it with?

Chapter 12: Thursday Morning

"*Have* you ever been to the Blowing Rock Horse Show?" Tucker asked Graves as they parked in the gravel parking lot at the L. M. Tate Show Grounds.

"I've taken visitors to the Hunters and Jumpers show in August a few times but not to this American Saddlebred Week. Did you know it started in 1923 when two guys raced from Green Park Inn to downtown Blowing Rock to out in the country? Now, Green Park Inn's under new management and a horse wouldn't be allowed to race in town. My wife likes to get out now and then and would love to go to the Boots and Saddles Ball. You?"

"No. Like most people, I don't visit what's in my back yard." Tucker adjusted the light jacket he wore to hide his gun. At the entrance, Tucker handed over the ten dollars to pay the fees for himself and Graves to enter. He probably could have flashed his badge to get in free, but it was for a good cause.

They parked and walked to the sand practice ring where half a dozen competitors took their horses through paces. The riders sat in a low buggy behind the horse and wore either a bright blue or a red satin bomber jacket with large black numbers on a white background pinned to their backs. They worked the horse through vocals, long reins and an oversized whip which they used to merely tap the horse. All the horses had shiny coats as well as combed mains and tails. Tucker couldn't tell for sure, of course, but the horses seemed to enjoy the workouts.

They passed the grandstand with its white railings, green metal roof and red, white and blue trappings then found the information booth with a dozen trophies on display on a table outside the booth. While waiting for help, Tucker read the inscriptions on some of the trophies. One of the larger silver bowls intrigued him.

"Tell me about this trophy," he asked when an official greeted him.

"The Challenge Trophy is awarded each year to the winner of the amateur five-gaited event. If the same person wins three years in a row, they get to keep the trophy. This one was donated years ago by the William Portsmith family." He suppressed a smile.

"Is that unusual?"

"No, but the ex-wife may get to keep it this year. She's won two years in a row. Her event comes up in a couple of hours."

"Where can I find her?"

The official consulted his clipboard. "She's probably grooming her horse in bay sixteen of stable seven." He pointed the way as an announcement broadcast the winners of the latest event.

"Where are her competitors stabled?" Tucker jotted down the locations.

"What do you know about saddlebred horses?" Graves asked as they walked the gravel road up the hill.

"They're supposed to be a treat to show. Beautiful, with extra long tails. Big friendly eyes. I think they have two gaits unique to the breed."

"I'm impressed."

Tucker nodded to a rider on horseback being led to the ring by a trainer. The two-step of the trainer mingled with the four-step clomp of the horse following down the hill. Tucker imagined the rider going over what was about to happen with reminders to keep his heels down, reins taut, back straight and eyes ahead of the horse.

Tucker slowed when they reached the number seven stable. A few of the stalls were empty but most had horses who watched the two men walk by. No other people were around. A freshly groomed black horse occupied bay sixteen. The hay smelled like newly cut grass. The men walked around the stable to the other side but saw only one woman working. It wasn't Tammy.

"Owning and showing a horse looks like a lot of work," Graves said.

Tucker nodded. "I've seen how much work trail horses are at Blue Falls Ranch. Double that for these horses. Transporting and handling show horses requires a devotion of sorts." Tucker nodded down the hill at one of the rings. "Their lives revolve around the shows. It's a lifestyle, not a hobby."

They checked the location of two of her competitors but didn't see Tammy until they found the third.

Tammy appeared to be intently studying a muscle in the chestnut's hind leg. Then Tucker saw the syringe.

"I wouldn't do that if I were you," Tucker said as he snapped a picture. "Intent carries a lesser sentence."

Tammy stood but had nowhere to go.

Graves said nothing but opened a paper bag for her to drop in the syringe.

"This isn't what it looks like. I saw the syringe lying in the hay."

Tucker couldn't imagine an owner dropping a syringe but kept a straight face. "Do we need to contact this horse's owner?"

Sweat formed on her forehead. "I'd rather not." Tammy walked out of the stall and closed the gate. "She is beautiful, isn't she?"

"So's the one you were to ride. This is out of our jurisdiction." Tucker looked at Graves as if he had a hard decision. "We'll have to cuff you while we call the local police." He looked back at Tammy. "They'll come blazing in here with sirens. But if you come along voluntarily, I'll let you tell the official why you have to drop out of today's competition." Tucker kept his face sympathetic while selling the fabrication. Press the advantage and hope for a confession in his own turf —the interrogation room.

Her shoulders drooped. "Thank you for being discrete." They followed her to her horse where she picked up her belongings. "What about my car? I can't leave it here overnight."

"We'll send someone for it."

"Family emergency," she told the official and made arrangements for her horse to return to the boarding section of the stable.

***

"I'm not used to feeling hair around my face." Jemma pulled open the door to the RAMs Rack charity resale shop and let Juanita enter first. "The men's clothes are on the left—that's where I get my work clothes. I don't know much about the women's section."

"The dresses are against the wall." Juanita led the way. "You stand still and let me hold some up against you."

Jemma stood as told, then used her arms to drape the selections while Juanita kept picking out dresses that Jemma never would have looked at, too many flowers, too short, sleeves not long enough, too low cut. Of the six dresses Jemma tried on, two looked like possibilities, according to Juanita who said she could adjust the length. On anyone else, they would go to the ankles but Juanita would take them up to Jemma's knees. Three skirts, two too-short pants to be shortened to knee length shorts, and three blouses later, Jemma followed Juanita to the back to try on shoes. They failed to find any that fit but did find a canvas bag. Juanita lingered over some brightly colored wedges. "Try those on. If they fit, I'll get them for you."

Juanita squealed and chattered in Spanish.

They fit and Jemma took them and her clothes to the check out counter.

"I'll be sitting over there," she pointed to a chair near the front door. "Now, it's your turn. My treat. Get yourself a couple of dresses and skirts for fun then some better work clothes. This is a 'thank you' for today but I'll pay you to make the alterations to my clothes."

Juanita headed for just the right spot on the dress rack. Jemma sat; shopping was more tiring than grooming horses. She called out to one of the photography club members who entered, "Hello Leslie."

"I didn't recognize you." Leslie quickly glanced around the shop. "You cut your hair."

Leslie's ashamed to be shopping in a thrift store, Jemma mused then shook her head so her hair swung side to side, becoming more accustomed to the cut by the moment.

"It looks lovely. What does your mother say?" A too sweet smile followed.

"My mo ... She likes it. Everyone thinks the cut's long overdue." Why the reference to her mother? Motherhood must be Leslie's whole identity.

"I remember when my daughter cut her hair short. She was in college. It was a sad day for me. They grow up too fast." She held up a bag. "These are some of her things. Last time she came to visit, she told me to empty her drawers and donate everything."

"I bet you miss her."

"She and her brothers have their own lives now. My husband and I are very proud of them." Leslie looked into the bag, then closed it. "I'm suffering from empty nest syndrome, I'm afraid."

Juanita come up carrying a bright skirt and coordinating blouse, and Jemma re-introduced them since they only met on Monday at supper. "Is that all you found?" Jemma said to Juanita. "Go back and get something else."

"More?"

Jemma nodded. Juanita grinned and headed back to the racks. "Alma wants to know your ideas about keeping deer out of the garden."

"Oh, my. Nothing is fool proof and the deer population is increasing." Leslie shook her head but smiled. "They'll jump a six foot fence with no problem. Bird netting works for a small area but it has to be rolled back every time you work the garden. The deer poke their nose into it and shy away."

"I think my cats would turn the whole net-thing into a playground." Visions of JK and DT rolling and getting caught in a tangle stopped the netting idea cold.

"Deer don't eat chives. She could ring a small garden with them but be careful they don't take over the garden." Leslie closed her eyes and thought a moment. "Has she tried sprinkling plants with pepper, garlic and cumin or putting hair clippings around? Deer don't like the human odor."

"That didn't work. She also had, um, the wranglers pee around the edges. They enjoyed that but the deer kept coming." Leslie's look of disgust told Jemma she'd been a little crude in her description. "She needs something simple that doesn't have to be reapplied after every rain." Maybe Leslie's gardening skills weren't any better than Alma's.

"The only other suggestion is a commercial product. Sorry I couldn't be of more help to your aunt. We had such a lovely supper at your ranch."

Leslie dropped off the donation bag at the desk and said she'd see Jemma tonight at Aaron's. Jemma had to explain "empty nest" to Juanita on the way home. Latinos don't suffer from that, Juanita announced. Most are happy to be free again.

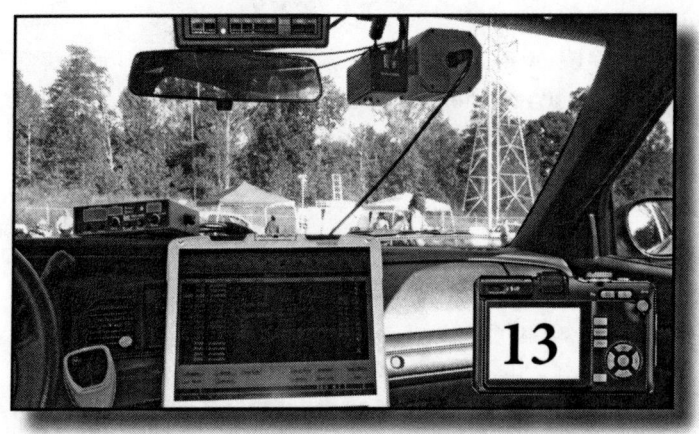

Chapter 13: Thursday Afternoon

Tammy sat silently in the back seat of the squad car during the twenty minute ride to the Law Enforcement Center, her arms tightly crossed over her chest as if she were holding herself together. Tucker and Graves had decided to forgo the handcuffs. When asked if she wanted a lawyer, she shook her head. Graves called in their status and used the computer to relay pertinent information.

Tucker glanced in the rearview mirror and saw that her face had turned very pale. Hoping to stave off her fainting, he asked her the only question he could think of to keep her engaged. "Your photographs of horses are great. What's your secret?"

She blinked a couple of times. "What did you say?"

"Any tips on photographing horses?"

Tammy cleared her throat and sat up straighter. "Shoot them from eye level or below to keep the legs from appearing short."

"Anything else?"

"Put a little baby oil or Vaseline on the muzzle and

around the eyes to make the skin look dark and velvety." Her voice strengthened. "Use a telephoto lens and stand ten to fifteen feet away. It makes the nose stand out less."

Five minutes left of the drive.

Graves entered the conversation. "Does that work for people, too?"

"I would imagine so. If you want a little action in the shot, focus on the scene and let the horse walk into it. To highlight the contours, have the sun behind you and take the photo with the shadow off to the side and somewhat forward."

Tucker parked and escorted Tammy from the parking lot into the Law Enforcement Center, thankful her color had returned and she had no trouble walking on her own. Once in the interrogation room, Tucker opened a thick folder, removed the top page and slid a copy of a newspaper article to her side of the table. "What do you know about this?"

She stared at the folder with her name on it then glanced at the clipping of the horse doping dated last year. "Nothing. I wasn't near that side of the stables before the show. My videos prove that. They are stamped with a date and time. I already told the Blowing Rock Police when they questioned me."

Tucker paused to show he didn't believe her. "Those dates can be manually adjusted."

"They can?" She frowned. "I didn't know that. Besides, Scott confirmed my story to the police. He saw me taking videos."

Tucker pulled a photo out of the folder and slid it to Tammy. "Poor Scott. He had a knack for photographing people in unusual situations. You saw some of his photos at last month's meeting. He showed them to the whole group, didn't he?" He rested his hand on the folder, indicating more evidence.

"His photo showed me at the horse show, getting ready for the competition. As you can see in the photo, I was putting a pen in my pocket. Nothing more." Tammy pointed to a spot in the picture.

Tucker looked closely at the photo and wished they had located Scott's mini laptop. "What do you think showed up when we zoomed in?"

Sweat beaded on her forehead. "I would never harm a horse. As a nurse, I know too much about meds and dosage to do that."

He shot back. "How easy is it to give too strong a dose? People make mistakes all the time."

Tammy looked at the two-way mirror, then at Tucker. She closed her eyes and frowned. When she opened her eyes, Tucker knew she'd made a decision. "Look, I admit to the horse. I may have given him too much but he didn't die. I had nothing to do with Scott. I swear."

Tucker hoped for more and kept questioning her. "Why take the photographer trophy?"

"It was an impulse and I've regretted it ever since. I couldn't figure out a way to return it." Tammy rubbed her forehead. "I know it's no excuse, but after my divorce, my husband turned our grown son against me. My life became focused on work, horses and photography. Scott was dead and didn't need the trophy."

"Go on."

"I had hoped it would inspire me to take better photos, like a talisman or good luck charm. All it did was add to my sense of failure. Please apologize to Scott's parents for me. The trophy will be more important to them now that their son is gone."

Three hours of circular questioning later, she kept to the same story. So far, all they had was horse related and no confession about Scott. She'd be out on bail soon enough, but at least this would give him probable cause to search her place and car for the laptop. Her lawyer would probably advise her to plead guilty and take a light sentence for the horse doping.

***

Jemma slipped into the meeting at Aaron's house a few minutes late Thursday evening. This presentation had better be worth the time since she'd miss the square dancing at the ranch tonight. To balance out partners, she usually took the man's part in the dancing because male guests had a tendency to be scarce on dancing night.

Although Juanita assured her the short cowboy boots went with the new skirt and blouse, the air on Jemma's bare legs and around her neck tingled with discomfort as well as excitement at daring to do something different to her body, her identity.

Aaron's face lit up and he clapped with glee at her entrance. "Lovely, just lovely." He rushed over to escort her to a seat. After she sat, careful to keep her knees together, he kissed the back of her hand. "Enchanté."

"Love the hair," Summer called from her position on the sofa.

"The woman has legs." Harold nudged her with his elbow from his seat next to her. Leslie smiled and nodded to her.

Flustered and pleased, Jemma stood and curtsied to the small group.

"About time," the judge added.

"My fans can reach me through Facebook. In the meantime, Aaron has a program for us." Jemma nodded to Aaron, both pleased and embarrassed at the reaction to her improved appearance.

"As I said on Monday when we were interrupted by poor Scott's demise," he briefly lowered his head in respect, "I believe this house has a haint. These photographs hint at the possibility. These were shot on a moonless night. See that shape at the top of the stairs?"

He moved the arrow to a spot on the PowerPoint projection circling an egg shaped bright area, not at all a round one sometimes caused by a camera flash. Aaron forwarded to the next photo.

"It's brighter here." The image was larger and the strongest in the fourth shot then faded and disappeared by the seventh one. "I set the camera to rapid fire." He turned on the lights in the room darkened by heavy drapes. "What do you think?"

Jemma involuntarily glanced at the stairs to the right. Although it was still daylight, the mountain behind the house brought early twilight through the upstairs window. Aunt Alma would believe him. So would every member of her UFO group.

"It's a hoax. Has to be." Harold stood and stretched his back.

"I knew you'd say that." Aaron passed around eight by ten copies of the photos. "Look at them. Inspect closely. I dare you to find anything altered or fashioned or—"

"Computer programs do wonders with photos these days," Harold interjected then looked to the judge for confirmation.

"We have had a case or two where altered photograph were submitted for evidence. We called in some experts and dismissed them."

Aaron squared his shoulders. "I've invited her—at

least, I think it is a her—to join us tonight."

Harold snorted. The judge asked, "How did you do that?"

"My momma's spirit board."

"Tool of the devil, my parent's preacher says." Summer crossed her arms over her chest.

"Where's the spirit board? I'd like to try it." Harold smirked at Summer.

Aaron pulled out the three foot square piece of plywood from behind his chair and propped it up in front of him.

Jemma was about to go and inspect the board when the judge stood.

"That chili smells good."

Aaron threw up his hands. "Let's eat first." Aaron led them to the kitchen. "Everyone grab a bowl. Line up by the pot on the stove and take some cornbread. My mamma always put corn in the cornbread so don't panic if you chomp down on something."

Jemma'd have to tell Alma that variation on cornbread, she thought while picking up a spoon and napkin. She vowed not to spill anything on her new outfit.

"Wonder what happened to Tammy?" Aaron ladled chili into bowls. "She worked so hard on poor Scott. I admire that she stuck with him and kept trying to bring him back to life."

Jemma didn't say a word.

"She could have been tied up at the stables with the horse show this week," Summer said. "Winning that trophy's become almost an obsession with her."

"Don't pick on her." Aaron pointed a spoon at Summer. "After what she tried to do for Scott, she deserves our respect. Imagine being immersed in injury and sadness all day."

"As opposed to what you do, tending to people's mouths? They both are healing arts," Jemma pointed out.

Leslie blew on a spoonful of chili to cool it then tasted. "Delicious. I'll have to get the recipe."

"Maybe your resident spirit wasn't buried properly, that's why she stays around." Harold dropped some shredded cheese on top of his chili. "My body's going to science. I wanted to be thrown on the compost pile and be given back to nature. Let them eat me since I ate them to keep alive all these years. The wife vetoed that idea."

"I understand there's a zero-emissions process that uses potassium hydroxide which leaves the body in a liquid and powdery white mass." Jemma bit into a piece of cornbread.

"Where in the world did you hear about something like that?" Harold asked.

"You don't have to sound so surprised." Jemma sipped tea and swallowed. "My aunt Alma told me about it. It's called Resomation, I believe."

"My parents would want me to have a proper burial." Summer looked around the group. "I'd prefer to be cremated and have my ashes thrown off of Grandfather Mountain and drift, sort of like a last hang glide."

Aaron added some chili to Harold's bowl. "Sounds better than the whole embalming process of filling your veins with formaldehyde to preserve the look, then sealing a casket so you are frozen in time in case anyone ever wants to dig you up." He looked at Summer. "Honey, I like your scatter the ashes idea better."

"I thought I was too young to think about it, but Scott's death shows it could happen at any time." Jemma wondered what her parents wanted, Aunt Alma,

Bo. Maybe it was time to find out their feelings. "What about you, Leslie?"

"Me?" Leslie looked up from the bowl she'd been studying. "I'm a good Catholic so I'll be buried on the church grounds."

"Not in your garden?" Harold asked.

"Heavens no. That wouldn't be proper." Leslie lifted her chin as if instructing heathens.

"Hear, hear." The judge patted Leslie's shoulder. "I agree with Leslie. Put me with the rest of my ancestors. That's what Scott's family has planned."

After supper, Harold put the spirit board on the coffee table. It was old, painted by hand on a square piece of plywood. The inch and a half red letters formed a large circle with a smaller inner circle of numbers in green. A slightly smaller circle indicated the degrees in black.

Aaron realigned the board. "The 'no' must head north; the 'yes' must head south. My grandparents got that in the 50s when Grandad was stationed in England after World War Two. It's a copy of the one designed by the Spiritualist Church." Aaron placed a down-turned glass on the tan circle in the middle. "My great-great grandmother's snuff came in this jar. It should be a good medium to channel my ghost."

The six settled in chairs and on the sofa surrounding the coffee table. Aaron took a deep breath and signaled for everyone to do the same. They exhaled slowly in unison.

"Get comfortable and put the index finger of your dominant hand lightly on this glass bottom."

Summer touched the glass and jumped up. "I can't do this. My Baptist upbringing."

"That's okay," Aaron said. "You can take notes on this

pad. List the questions and answers. Some get spelled out if they can't be answered with a simple 'yes' or 'no.' Leslie, what about you?" Aaron inflected a hint of dare into his question.

Leslie tapped the glass. "My faith is strong enough to handle this."

Summer looked at the door, plainly wanting to leave. Instead she sat and perched the pad on her knee.

After the remaining five's index fingers rested on the glass, Aaron asked in a calm tone, "Is anybody there, please? Is anybody there?"

Nothing happened and he said, "Please let us know if anybody is there."

Slowly the glass moved to "yes."

"Please tell us your name."

As the glass moved, Jemma looked at the other participants trying to tell if one of them purposely moved the glass. Harold frowned, Aaron concentrated, the judge smirked and Leslie stared at the glass. Summer watched intently with pen poised to write.

The glass moved to "I" then spelled out "Iris."

"Do you have a message for anyone here?"

The glass moved south to "yes."

"Who?"

It spelled out "all." Jemma resisted the urge to remove her finger, especially when she saw Leslie's finger shake.

"What is the message?"

Everyone spelled the answer aloud "death."

"I wonder if that means how she died?" Aaron said, "Tell us."

"Tainted food" was quickly spelled. Jemma thought that was the complete message and was about to remove her finger when the glass kept moving.

"W-A-R-N"

Leslie jerked away her finger and grabbed her stomach. "Where's the bathroom?"

Aaron pointed to the back of the house. "As host, I should have pointed out those when you arrived. There's another one up the stairs and to the right."

Jemma's stomach lurched as Leslie disappeared into the bathroom. They all looked up the stairs. Was that a shadow? Jemma moved first and headed up the stairs. Haint or not, her supper was coming back up. After she emptied her stomach and washed her face, she stopped at the top of the stairs, not sure if her stomach had settled enough. Retching sounds came from the kitchen below.

Jemma opened an upstairs door and found a telephone. She punched in 9-1-1 on the phone beside the bed and reported possible poisoning. She hung up the phone and looked around the room. No wonder he kept the door closed. Framed photographs of local women lined his dresser. Wasn't that the judge's wife? She recognized a couple of the others, all married women. Her stomach groaned, she ran out, careful to close Aaron's bedroom door behind her, and made a second trip to the toilet. The chili was as bad coming up as it was good going down.

Wait until Tucker hears of this, she thought, after washing her face and rinsing her mouth. No. She couldn't call him. He'd kissed someone else and she hadn't sorted out how to react. It hurt, no doubt about that.

The first responders came in the front door and Jemma made her way down the stairs. The others gathered in the living room as two ambulances pulled in. The room was so crowded that Jemma and her EMT moved to the front porch. Detectives that Jemma recognized but didn't know arrived and the food was confiscated for evidence. Even Aaron had thrown up. The sick were loaded into ambulances and transported to the Watauga Medical Center's Emergency room. All Jemma knew was that the ride while laying on her back, swaying side to side with the turns, answering questions for the EMT with her stomach churning was the longest in her life. "Tainted food," kept replaying in her head.

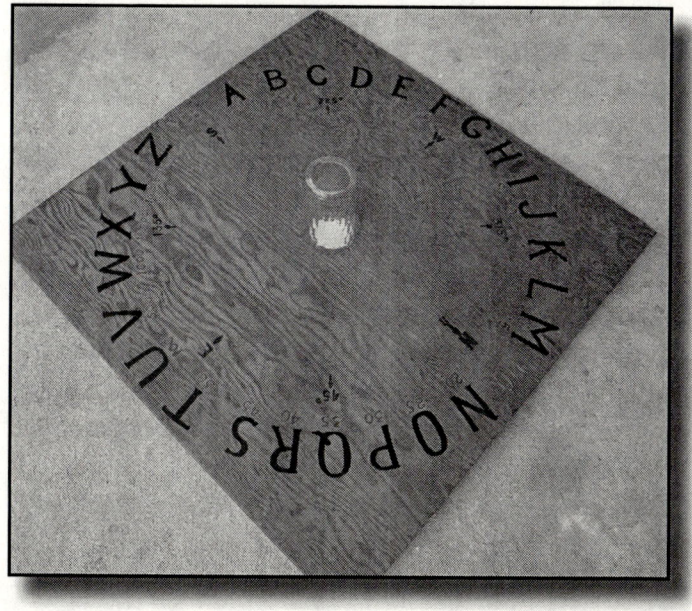

Chapter 14:
Late Thursday & Early Friday Morning

Tucker settled in the chair next to Jemma's hospital bed. He pulled out his notebook and wrote a few notes about the events at Aaron's house while she slept.

He'd arrived after the ambulance had left, talked with the detectives on scene and read their reports. Jemma could fill in the blanks in the morning. He glanced at her while mulling over the reports. Something was different about her, besides the hospital gown. He stood and leaned over her, reluctant to touch and awaken her. He chanced brushing hair away from her face.

She'd cut her hair. That long, beautiful hair that he'd unbraided a time or two. She'd said it was heavy, a hassle to wash. It took forever to dry. Once he'd asked her why she didn't cut it but she didn't have an answer. Long or short wasn't his call. Her choice. She always looked great to him. Sleeping, she appeared so vulnerable. He hadn't even been around to protect her. He'd been with Wanda. Talk about opposites. Wanda was tiny, energetic and ambitious. She had an insatiable appetite for food, for life, for more.

Jemma loved life in a different way. She'd jump first and then deal with the consequences. Hard work didn't faze her but it didn't make her rich either. Money was somewhere on her list but not near the top.

Ah, Jemma. Why was he so attracted to her? He went to the sink and threw water on his face then returned to his chair.

She'd lied to him, told half-truths when they first met. Two things his father had never tolerated. As a kid, one lie and he was punished. It didn't matter if it was about being finished with homework or his liking the corn pudding. A lie was a lie. Then Wanda had entered his world, became his world for a short time. He'd avoided lying in his personal life ever since, no matter the temptation. Work was different. Justice could sometimes be served through his acting skills.

Family tales had his dad home from the Viet Nam war with two vultures on his shoulders—drink and pot. He'd had to stay in his parents' barn until he escaped their clutches. He'd spent days in the woods asking himself questions, getting his body fit and losing his desire to escape himself. His father found his version of truth, married Tucker's mom and lived an honorable life ever since.

His mom claimed that thoughts of her had carried him through the jungle fighting and made him regain his soul. When he lived in the barn, she'd see him every day, flirt, wear a push-up bra and vee neck blouse. Nothing overt, mind you, just enough to keep him on the trail to her. She claimed it was the push-up bra her mother gave her that did the trick. He had hard, life changing choices to make and she'd made sure he didn't possum out on her, no drug-induced sleepy head for her.

Tucker yawned and stretched out his back.

What about tonight? Should he tell Jemma he was in Wanda's hotel room at the time of the call? Should he mention the picnic that led to the hotel room? Graves would advise that he could wait to see if she asked where he was, a variation on the "don't ask, don't tell" line of reasoning. Or he could tell her and cauterize the wound, so to speak. Which was better? To hurt her now or chance hurting her in the future should she find out.

Tucker's cell phone vibrated around five in the morning with a pre-set to wake him. Jemma still slept when he left to get ready for work.

***

Jemma woke, hungry and ready to return home but the hospital doctor wouldn't be around for a few hours. After eating everything on her tray, she found Leslie's room; the others were ahead of her. Their one-size-fits-all hospital gowns completely engulfed Leslie and Summer but were short and tight on the rest of them.

"It's a relief to see you," Aaron said. "We hoped all of us survived my chili. I swear I followed my mother's recipe which I've made many times. All my ingredients were fresh; the only thing different was that I used some spicy beans from ..." Aaron glanced around at all of them, but it seemed his gaze lingered on the judge. "A friend."

Jemma wondered if he got the beans from the judge, or maybe from the judge's wife; after all her photo was among the ones in Aaron's bedroom. "It tasted great, the best chili I've ever had. Honest. I'd like to give the recipe to Alma for the ranch."

Aaron's smile failed.

"You didn't do this to make us believe the Spirit board?" Summer asked.

"Don't even joke about it." Aaron turned to the judge. "I feel so awful. Will they have to cancel court?"

"No. I'm not on the schedule this week. Am I the only one that realizes we were almost killed?" The judge looked at each of them, Jemma last.

"You mean on purpose? Did anyone say what it was?" Harold asked.

"Not yet." Leslie pushed away her tray, leaving most of the food.

"You don't want that?" Jemma needed to make up for last night's lost meal.

"My appetite isn't what yours is. Help yourself." Leslie adjusted the sheet and thin blanket on the bed.

Jemma grabbed a half piece of toast and passed the plate. Maybe Leslie had received a larger dose. The judge was her age but much larger and had taken a piece of toast, so his appetite had returned.

"We should ask the spirit board," Summer said.

Jemma graciously did not mention that Summer had refused to use the sprit board.

"The judge asked a question, and I have one," Harold said. "Which of us did this?"

"I swear it wasn't me. I'm relieved it wasn't bad cooking." Aaron backed up. "Whoever did this must have killed Scott."

Everyone else stepped back from Leslie's bed. Jemma dropped the last crumb of toast onto the tray. "One of us" had an appetite suppressing ring to it.

"We were only sickened. It could have been an accident. We don't know yet," Summer pleaded. "I hate to think one of us would have a reason to murder a friend."

"Don't kid yourself," the judge said. "The slimmest of reasons are enough for some people. Jealousy, old wounds, secrets, too many drinks, fender bender."

"I don't have any secrets," Jemma said. "My family's too close and too perceptive. Aunt Alma can root out anything I would try to hide."

"Nothing you're ashamed of?" The judge stood at the door.

"Some minor infractions I long ago came to terms with. How about you, Harold?" Jemma asked. He played with guns, hunted four-legged animals but once hunted the two-legged kind for his country. Why not make a little side money or knock off a pesky neighbor?

"Anyone who has lived as long as I have has some regrets." Harold walked to the window. He'd put on his pants before visiting Leslie but the hospital gown gapped and exposed his hairy back. "My army days were rough, my wife was forced to move a lot. I used to wonder why she stayed with me. Now? These are the good years. I wouldn't jeopardize that by poisoning someone."

"I lead a simple life teaching at ASU. No motive here." Summer stepped closer to the door.

"I have all kinds of secrets. What's the fun of life without mystery?" Aaron flexed his wrist with a feminine flair but the humor fell flat.

"I'm a wife and mother. My family is my life." Leslie's hand shook as she smoothed the sheet and blanket over her legs in the bed.

"What about before you met your husband?" Jemma thought of her Aunt Alma's younger days. "In your late twenties, early thirties. What was your career?"

"All I ever wanted to be was a mother, to love and raise my children." Leslie pulled the covers up higher to cover her heart.

"We're all innocent. Maybe the ghost did it," the judge

said, the first to leave the room.

Jemma returned to her room and called home. "What did Tucker say about your hair?" was the second question Alma asked after inquiring about her health.

"He hasn't been by." Jemma tried to keep the worry out of her voice. He had to still care. "The ambulance carted me off last night before he arrived. He probably had to work on Scott's case until late."

"You don't need to make excuses for him. We're packing the picnic for Whiskey Ridge. Do you want your dad or mom to fetch you? They were by last night but you were asleep."

"No. The judge's wife will drive us back to Aaron's house to pick up our cars. Sorry I'm missing the trail ride today."

"Don't worry about the guests. Bo and Miguel are joshing each other over who's boss. Juanita wants to know if the skirt you wore last night needs cleaning."

"I managed to keep my clothes out of the line of fire. Tell her my new look created a sensation last night. Today, we have to go by the law enforcement office and make statements again."

"Juanita says to remember to wear the necklace. The bright colors show off your shape."

Jemma showered, washed her chin length hair and was ready to go moments after the doctor released them. Someone had put harmless syrup of ipecac in the chili.

Chapter 15: Friday Morning

"**Strike** two, Tucker. Tammy may be guilty of shooting up a horse but she wasn't involved last night." The Chief thrust Tucker a pile of papers. "Time to dig deeper."

Tucker and Graves returned to the conference room and divided their notes and reports into stacks relating to each of the remaining suspects.

Graves emptied the contents of a bag he'd brought in with him onto a corner of the long table. "Thought you needed to add to your collection. The ceramic rooster stands for the judge."

The judge had a good life, as far as Tucker could see. A wife he loved, plenty of income and benefits, enough respect to keep being re-elected. Maybe boredom had turned him to gambling on cockfights to keep his juices going.

Tucker held up a girl doll dressed in sportswear. "Is this Summer?"

"She photographs athletic women."

Maybe Tucker should take Summer up on that fitness evaluation, he thought, tapping his stomach. His eating habits could use a change.

"The tuxedoed man doll is for Aaron. Either because he dresses up or because he prefers men. Your choice."

Aaron wasn't local so Tucker had no history to draw on. His gut told him Aaron put on a show, too much of one, as if he hid something important.

Tucker put the fake flower on Leslie's stack of papers, the shot glass on Scott's.

"The cat's for Jemma since the horse represents Tammy."

"Who's this for?" Tucker pointed to a rubber alligator.

"Guess."

"Then, where's your figure?"

Graves reached into his pocket and pulled out a plastic policeman.

"Since we're all here, let's use this to track ourselves a killer." Tucker grabbed the notes on the judge and reviewed everything in detail, looking for something they'd missed. If memory served, the judge had an alcoholic father and a pushy mother who made him go to law school. He couldn't make it as a lawyer and was a fair judge. His wife was from a well-to-do family.

Later when Graves came back with fresh coffee, Tucker looked at the piles and said, "It all comes down to secrets and lies." He stood, stretched and leaned back. "I've been sitting too long."

"Is Jemma speaking to you yet?"

"She hasn't had a chance. I left this morning before she woke up."

"Chicken." Graves picked up the ceramic rooster and waggled it.

"No, I had to get here to fill in the chief." Tucker put the spirit board near the figures on the conference table and looked at it as if it would tell him the name of the murderer.

Graves followed Tucker's lead and stood and shook out his legs. "Most lies don't involve the law; they're social niceties. You've never lived with a woman and don't understand the 'Do I look fat in this?' question. The answer is 'no' or 'I like the other dress better.'" Women take things personal, even when we don't intend it that way."

"She cut her hair." He put the Jemma cat on the east edge of the spirit board looking in.

"Good thing you left. I know how you liked it long. At least you didn't have a chance to tell her the truth." Graves stretched his hands over his head.

"It looked fine. She looked good." He arranged some of the figures on the board, putting Scott's shot glass in the center.

"Did you see Wanda last night?" Graves put the alligator and policeman on the north arrow next to "No."

"For a while before the call came in about a possible link in poisonings. I'm due to see Wanda again tonight. She leaves Sunday." When he tried to stand up the two dolls, the one for Aaron fell on top of the other.

"Are you going to tell Jemma?"

Tucker dropped into a chair beside the spirit board and returned his attention to Graves. "How about I tell you about Wanda? You can advise me." No one knew about this part of his past but Tucker felt the need to finally tell someone. Graves had earned his trust.

Graves sat, leaned back and nodded.

"I was in my twenties, driving down Blowing Rock Road and slammed on my brakes to avoid hitting the car in front of me as it swerved into the corner gas station. I saw a girl holding up a sign for a five dollar car wash and turned in behind the car I had almost hit. The woman, not a girl, wore short shorts and a T-shirt that was damp in the hot sun."

"Let me guess," Graves said. "You were twenty-five and had left behind girls and their silly conversations about clothes, hair or music. Now that you were an adult, you were ready for a woman. You knew life was serious, that you could improve the world in some small way. What was the cause the fund raiser was for?"

Tucker frowned. Had he been so predictable at that age? "Humane Society. I stopped the car to talk with an attendant when the woman at the curb handed over her sign to someone else. Is she leaving?' I asked without thinking first. The attendant turned in the direction I was looking.

"Hey Wanda," he yelled and motioned her over. "This one's for you."

"She shook her head. No more for me after this. I've got to get some lunch.' Wanda held out her hand. Five dollars, please. Or more, depending on how you feel about our four-legged friends.'

"I gave her a ten, a lot of money to me in those days, rolled up the windows and stepped out of the car. She looked around for help and two young men came over with a hose, buckets and sponges." Tucker stopped.

"That's your big secret?" Graves threw down his pen and pushed back his chair.

Tucker's heart beat too fast, almost as if he were on a witness stand. He drew in a deep breath and continued. "She winked at me and said, 'I'm better at drying off since I can't reach the top of the car.' " She stepped back a couple of feet to avoid the spray and I followed her and told her my name.

"'Hunk didn't seem appropriate,' she said, then laughed. 'Maybe stud since we're raising money to help animals. Oh, come on, you know you're cute.'

"Not as cute as you.' I surprised myself with that fast come back.

"She looked down at her wet tennis shoes and said, 'You should see me when I try to dress up.'

"'It's a deal. When can I pick you up for dinner?'

"'No, I can't do that.' She put her hands on her hips, unintentionally emphasizing her curves.

"She broke my heart with that, then she returned to my car and used a towel to wipe off the windows. I couldn't help myself and I said, 'At least let me take you to lunch. You planned to eat after cleaning my car.'

"'That's true.' She wiped off the hood, headlights and bumper before taking another towel to dry the sides and trunk.

"I stood by and watched, mesmerized by her twisting and bending to reach the various car parts."

Graves leaned in closer to Tucker. "I'm drooling here like a blue tic hound."

"Her butt was in constant motion for the ten minutes it took to dry the car. She'd stretch to reach a spot, balancing on one foot, then sit on her haunches with her knees spread to reach parts of the fender." Tucker paused and licked his lip.

"Go on. Then what?"

Her T-shirt was wet by the time she was through so she draped the towel around her neck so it hung down, almost to her waist. "I might take you up on that lunch," she finally said before grabbing a gym bag from the gas station office. She also picked up the key to the women's restroom which was outside and around the side.

"I felt good at this point and leaned against my newly cleaned car to wait when she poked her head out of the lady's room.

"Oh, Tucker, can you bring me one of those clean towels?"

"When I knocked on the door with a towel, she grabbed me by the belt buckle and pulled me in. We never did have lunch that day." Tucker adjusted in his seat, feeling some relief at finally telling someone about meeting Wanda.

Graves grinned and shook his head. "You lucky dog, you. No wonder you hooked up with her again."

"Your advice is to keep it to myself?" Jemma had not told him much about her old boyfriends; neither had she hidden the existence of them.

"Leave me out. I'll go along with whatever you decide. Full disclosure is over-rated. What do you have to gain?" Graves finished his coffee and picked up some papers. "Great story but you couldn't give me the life of a single man."

The burden of keeping a long-held secret dissipated like salt in warm water. But, he hadn't told the whole story. The pressure of the secret no longer had a strangle hold on his conscience, more like a pinch hold.

"Speaking of single, let's look at Aaron's file again. Was the poison a warning? If so, for who? Why?" Tucker pulled a stack of papers to him.

Why was Scott killed? What did he know that put him in jeopardy? Tucker looked at the blow ups of the photographs from Scott's home computer. They'd printed a dozen of the thousands, concentrated on the ones of the photography club. In the photo, Aaron was seated next to a dental patient. He wore a mask, gloves and a paper smock. The sliver of the patient's face showed earrings and styled hair. Aaron held dental floss stretched between his two hands. Tools on the tray were shiny and ordinary. No smoking guns in that photo. He made a note to verify Aaron's dental license.

The one of Leslie held her in profile in front of a computer at Watauga Library. Tucker used a magnifying glass to see an old newspaper headline filled the monitor screen. "'Local Woman Still Missing.' Can you read the date below the headline?" He handed Graves the photo and magnifying glass.

Graves tried to read the date and the name of the newspaper but couldn't. "We'll get the tech guys to enhance the digital photo. Those wizards can come up with a name for us. Isn't one of her sons a lawyer down in Charlotte?"

"It doesn't look like a Watauga Democrat headline."

"Could be her daughter's boyfriend. Leslie would want to check up on him."

Tucker picked up Tammy's photo. How could he have been wrong about her? The photo showed her on horseback but he wasn't lucky enough to see a syringe hanging out of a pocket. Tucker didn't see anything out of the ordinary in the photo. The English saddle wasn't to his liking but it suited the jodhpurs and English boots and helmet. Under the magnifying glass, the riding crop looked standard.

"You can't let her go?"

"You remember the mistakes."

"Don't beat yourself up. In fifteen years, I can count on one hand your mis-calls. We have a slew of suspects.

We'll figure it out."

Another detective came into the conference room. "I've had a complaint involving one of your suspects. Harold Bench."

Tucker motioned him over.

"A single woman rented a cabin on the river near his place. She's new to the area, from California, and wanted a quiet place in the woods. On her second day, a man came by and asked permission to use the boulder in the river in front of her house. He wanted to fish."

Tucker, nodded, thinking it was polite of the man to ask. He'd probably fished there most days during fishing season.

"The next day, a scruffy looking man with one crossways eye knocked on her door and asked the same thing. The woman was becoming nervous but gave permission and then went to work in town."

"No laws broken there," Graves said.

"The following day, Harold stopped by, introduced himself, and asked the same thing. By now, the woman was thinking of a scene from the old Deliverance movie and decided to contact us."

"I can see where she's spooked. What do you plan to do?" Tucker had a good idea who the other two men were.

"Not much I can do except go by and talk with the men."

"We'll talk with Harold. Try not to rile up those other two. They've been hauled in for trespassing and poaching as well as drunk and disorderly. Wouldn't put it past them to be armed. Watch your back."

Chapter 16: Friday Afternoon

At Aaron's house, Jemma and Summer stayed and helped clean up while the judge, Harold and Leslie went on to the sheriff's office to sign their second statements in less than a week.

"Oh, good, we're alone. Girls, now we can talk." Aaron led Jemma to the sink and gave her some rubber gloves. "You need to start protecting those hands now that you've discovered a whole new you." He dampened a cloth and handed it to Summer to wipe up after he cleared the table and counters. "I'll start. Remember, dental hygienists are a little like hair stylists only people think because it's in a medical setting, it's confidential. Honey, we're not psychiatrists. There's no oath of silence involved."

Jemma ran water in the sink and waited for the suds to develop before putting in some bowls.

"Recently, there have been news leaks to the press for leads to follow up on, not by me, mind you, but it has happened. Poor Scott told me that. I do know that the judge sometimes brags about some of the sentences he's handed down. Also he flips a coin to make a decision. I wonder what other gambling habits he has?" Aaron talked more to Summer since Jemma's back was to them.

"I'm glad I've never been to court. What else do you know?" Summer dropped the eating utensils into the hot soapy water and returned to the table.

"He adores his wife, who married below her station, if you know what I mean. He'd be a slob if his wife didn't keep on him."

"Do you think he could have killed Scott?"

Jemma turned enough to look at the two of them, wanting to see Aaron as he answered.

His eyes widened then he shrugged. "Anything is possible. He's pragmatic and knows his way around the criminal world, such as it is in Boone.

"If he thought Scott messed with his wife, he could have done it. What do you think, Jemma?"

"Jealousy is a powerful emotion." Jemma returned to scrubbing, hoping to learn something she could pass on to Tucker.

"What do you know about Tammy?"

"She's still not over a nasty divorce."

"Do you think she still loves her husband?" Summer cleared her throat after asking.

"No. I'm sure of that much. She poured out the whole saga one night at Murphy's. I wish she'd put that mess behind her. She needs to loosen up, live beyond the past and that horse of hers."

"She keeps herself in good shape." Summer moved to the stove to clean and Jemma handed her a roll of paper towels, then leaned against the counter.

"Talk like that, girl, could get you into trouble." Aaron glanced at Jemma as if gauging her reaction.

"What's wrong with admiring athletes?" Summer addressed the question to Jemma.

"It's your business; dealing with athletes is your passion." Jemma wiped down the counter but angled her body so she could see the other two, the better to watch as well as hear the interplay.

"I admire her, too." Aaron said. "She got my attention on Monday."

"What about murder? Did she do it?" Summer let the question hang in the air.

"Anger, passion, knowledge of drugs. I say she could have." Aaron looked at Summer and Jemma. "I hope she didn't."

"What do you know about Leslie?" Jemma asked.

Aaron fished out two dry dish towels and handed one to Jemma.

"Bless her heart," Summer said. "She was devoted to her kids. The trouble is, she's lost without them. Reminds me of a workaholic, she doesn't know what to do with herself now that her duty's done."

"One time she let it slip that her kids told her they are too busy to spend an hour on the phone with her every day. She said it in a way that broke my heart." Aaron dried a bowl and put it in the cabinet. "I'm good about calling Momma on Sundays."

"Can you picture her as a cold-blooded killer?" Summer shook her head in answer to her own question.

"What about Harold?" Jemma and Aaron developed a rhythm in finishing the dishes.

"Loves his war stories," Summer said. "I appreciate what he did for us and this country but he's stuck in that Cold War era fighting mode. And yes, I think he could kill without hesitation."

They finished in the kitchen and went to the living room.

"It could have been worse," Aaron said after assessing that most of the mess had been in the kitchen.

"Yeah," Summer said, "we could have finished the chili."

Aaron swatted her with a dust cloth. "Or our ghost could have finished her message. What if she wasn't warning us about last night? What if her warning was for something coming up next?"

"I thought I saw something at the top of the stairs before we all got sick." Jemma rearranged some chairs.

"Where was your camera then? You could have corroborated my story."

"It was out of the corner of my eye, just a hint of a shadow."

"I tried to see the ghost that haunts East Hall at ASU one time." Summer swept the hardwood floor area vacated by the chairs. "We held a séance in the basement but she never showed up. We ended up having a party."

"I thought you avoided those anti-church things." Jemma smiled to temper her teasing. "Isn't there a ghost at the library at Lees-McRae College in Banner Elk?" Jemma worked on clearing the table used during the presentation.

"I know," Aaron closed up his laptop with the PowerPoint program. "We could have the mother of all séances and call up all the ghosts in the High Country. We could ask them what they wanted and release them from being trapped here."

Summer visibly shivered. "I don't want any part of that. You'd probably screw it up and double their power. I wasn't even twenty-one when I tried that stunt at East Hall. One ghost in your house is enough."

"I was funnin' you," Aaron said, rubbing her shoulder. "My, your arms are strong. We could leave the clean-up with Jemma and explore my bedroom."

Jemma turned to him. "I'll bet you only pretend to like men, you stinker." Then she looked at Summer. "And so do you."

Both of them opened and closed their mouths and the silence lasted many seconds.

Jemma raised her eyebrows and said, "Gottcha." She returned to cleaning the room. It didn't matter to her about sexual choices, but it mattered to their public images. The moment passed and the three finished cleaning up the house.

Jemma stopped for gas to let the other two arrive at the sheriff's office ahead of her. Signing another statement wasn't the problem. Facing Tucker was stickier. Competing for his "favor" didn't sit right, but what choice did she have? She wasn't walking away from the best man she'd had in her life.

Once at the sheriff's office, she ducked into the bathroom and combed her hair, admiring the sheen and cut. Her stomach tightened a bit, but not like last night with the ghost and the chili. She put on lip gloss and took a last look at the more glamorous woman in the mirror before walking past the former sheriffs' photo row and into the detectives' room.

Graves looked up and motioned her over. Her skirt swished as she strolled to his desk, conscious of Tucker's cubicle located beyond Graves'. The effect was wasted, she thought, when Tucker didn't poke his head around the cubicle walls.

"He's in with the chief," Graves said. "You'll have to settle for me. How are you feeling?"

"Fully recuperated." She looked at the chief's closed door before whispering, "Why didn't he come to see me in the hospital? I know you all are busy with the murder and the fake poisoning last night but he could have come by early this morning."

Graves pushed her statement over to her. "Be sure to read it carefully before you sign it."

"Sticking by your partner." Jemma sighed and read the statement.

When she picked up the pen to sign it, Graves said, "He likes your hair cut. Told me so first thing this morning."

Jemma sat up straighter and signed the form. It wasn't a ghost that visited her in her dreams last night. "Thanks, Graves." She leaned in. "Anything on the judge?"

Graves stood. "Thank you for coming in. By the way, I admire the new look, as my wife would say."

Jemma took the hint and left. At home, she changed clothes and called the kitties. The wranglers and most of the guests were out on the trail. Alma and Juanita wouldn't be back for a couple of hours since they were serving lunch up on Whiskey Ridge. She wasn't used to being around the ranch when it was so quiet. She walked around outside her cabin looking for JK and DT.

A baby-like cry drew Jemma up the mountain behind her cabin where her gray Russian Blue was high in the tree. Trapped ten feet up in the overlapping branches near a fork in a tree, Jemma Kitty struggled to free her hind legs.

"What have you gotten yourself into?" Jemma called up to the kitty.

The wind swayed the branches, slipping her tighter into the tree's grip. Her powerful hind legs weakened. She fought for freedom, tore out a claw, and kept trying. Her jammed back legs stopped moving and she yowled.

Jemma's heart pounded; panic closed her throat.

"Hold on Jemma Kitty! I'll be right back." Her voice came out in a whisper.

It took a ladder, a jack to pry apart the branches and courage for Jemma to face the terrified cat. While keeping balance on the ladder, she talked calmly to Jemma Kitty and tried to keep her own body from shaking. She pumped up the jack with one hand to spread the branches and supported the cat with the other. She released Jemma Kitty from the tree and hugged her to her chest to climb down the ladder. Jemma sat on the ground, trembling. She gently checked for broken bones and bleeding but found only damage to JK's hind claws.

When Jemma Kitty first tried to stand, her back legs splayed out behind her. She quickly regained control and groomed herself, staying close to Jemma. One life down, eight still around. Trapped by her own actions then trying to extract herself, her kitty had made things worse. Could something like that have led to Scott's murder?

Jemma tucked JK into the crook of the sofa and petted her for a while. She turned on her computer to take advantage of this rare two hours of quiet time during the afternoon. "I'll never let you outside again," she vowed to JK. "It's too dangerous." She googled Scott Barker and traced him to many places on the internet; after all, he'd photographed lots of people and had written some lead stories for the newspaper. He had a photography website where he sold his more artistic photographs. Jemma bookmarked the site for future reference.

She had some photos that were as good as some of those on the site. Maybe she should set up a website. Once it was set up, it shouldn't take much to keep it current. She already ran the ranch's site. She went to Facebook; she had "friended" him back when she joined the photo club a few months ago, but had never taken the time to look at his online photos or contacts. A lot of the club members were in his contact list but a few weren't. Harold and Leslie probably didn't do much on a computer. The judge was there, as was Summer, Aaron and Tammy.

She heard a truck pull in, went to the window and saw that Alma and Juanita had returned from the lunch cookout. She glanced at the clock on the computer and an hour had passed. She looked up Aaron's mother's house to see what part of Atlanta she lived in. According to tax records, it was an affluent neighborhood, which fit with what Aaron had said.

Tammy currently used her maiden name; her ex-husband wasn't mentioned on Facebook so Jemma couldn't look him up. She searched the public court records for Tammy's divorce but by the time she found it, she was running out of time. She traced his tax record off the mountain but still in North Carolina. He still owned the home they'd lived in so Tammy couldn't have taken him for much when she left him. Just because she wasn't at the chili incident, didn't mean she didn't have something against Scott. She could be guilty despite Aaron's admiration for her nursing skills. What better way to look innocent than to attempt to save someone? She and Aaron could be in cahoots.

Leslie and her husband had owned their current house for twenty-five years. Jemma tracked down two of Leslie's children on MySpace but their photos were all amateur and college related. No pictures of Mom and Dad. Harold didn't show up anywhere except the tax records.

Jemma googled "skip tracing" to find the sites to track down someone. Maybe she could work backwards. Any of them could have a secret from the distant past that had caught up with them. Scott could have found out something and planned to go public with it.

The clomp of horse hooves alerted her that the trail riders had returned. JK remained asleep, tucked into the corner of the couch.

Jemma greeted the riders and helped unsaddle the horses. "Any word on the next cockfight?" she asked Miguel when they were alone.

"Nada. I will let you know when I hear something. It is usually only one hour before."

Chapter 17: Friday Afternoon

Tucker forwarded the Alerts for Harold, Sunny and Tammy to Graves' inbox then concentrated on the ones he had for Aaron. Aaron had been chatty the past few days, especially on the ghost websites.

His own blog gave details about how he'd captured the ghost in photos, but he had to be contacted separately to get a copy. He did indeed attend high school and a dental hygiene program at a school in Atlanta. Aaron mentioned his momma a lot in earlier posts but not so much since the first of the year. Momma's boy cutting his own cord. Good for him.

Try as he might, Tucker couldn't find a link from or to Aaron on the gay sites. He could have used a pseudonym. He checked discussion sites but mainly found him commenting on a few women's sites. Tucker even smiled at one of Aaron's entries about the old song lyrics about getting out the back door.

"Graves, look at this."

Graves rolled his chair around the cubicle divider.

"Find something?"

"I'll bet our boy Aaron likes the girls, not the boys, as he led us and everyone else to believe. My guess is that he prefers married women. His affected feminine ways must have made it easy to get by the husbands."

"A wolf in sheep's clothing. We can find out who his regular dental clients are. Maybe one of them will tie into Scott or someone Scott knew. I'm glad he doesn't work for my dentist."

"Great secret. A man pretending to prefer men which puts both the wives and husbands at ease."

"No threat of a commitment. Guaranteed secrecy so he's free to attend to as many ladies as he wants. Perfect set up for a guy in his twenties."

"He's in his thirties now and distancing himself from Atlanta and his mother. I wonder if he's tiring of his lifestyle." Tucker swiveled away from the computer. "When Aaron's in his forties, wonder if his past will be a painful secret or will he make a joke of it and wear it like a badge of honor. He's had an unusual rite of passage."

"Scott could have found out about one or more of his affairs. Making them public would blow his cover of being gay. Men in the town would be forewarned and not let him near their wives." Graves rolled back to his desk.

Tucker's fingers paused on the keyboard. Back when he was twenty, thinking of Wanda had consumed him. He had managed to work, visit family and act normal but he hadn't felt normal. Everything related to her, getting to be with her.

Tucker rubbed his hands over his face. He had survived her one time. Now? Wanda was still tempting but he had changed. Wised up. He had become more comfortable with himself. She had been his rite of passage.

Then there was Jemma. The one he looked forward to talking to every night. The one who frustrated his every attempt to keep her out of investigating. The one he trusted even though she lied to him when she was in her CSI wannabe mode.

Without thinking, he googled Wanda under her married name. The business was her passion. She did charity works on behalf of pets and other animals. According to her blog, she worked sixty-hour weeks and loved what she did. No mention of a divorce. He searched for her under the name she gave him and found nothing. He searched court records but didn't see anything in the state records relating to a divorce. He then checked the husband who apparently didn't use computers except for his business. More than likely, he paid someone to keep up his website.

"Harold keeps up with his war buddies," Graves called out.

Tucker walked over to his partner's desk.

"He chats in detail about all the years overseas. He's telling stories to help one of the guys write a book."

Tucker studied the screen. "He likes his guns. Lots of technical details. I've seen him at the gun club."

"Harold's quick to verbally attack anyone who criticizes the war. He likes the idea of using the military to police the world. Curious that he left out a year in his stories while on active duty." Graves pointed to the dates on the screen.

"He could have been stateside and away from the action."

"I'll re-read some of those Facebook posts and look into any stories that seem like he's hiding something. Maybe he had one gunshot too many. When I followed up for the detective on the harassment of that girl by the river, he claimed that he was merely checking up on the new single woman and didn't know that the other two guys had been doing the same."

"He's supposed to be securely married." Almost five o'clock. Too late to cancel his date with Wanda. Somehow, he'd lost interest. He didn't care if she was still married or not. He'd meet her as planned, thank her for looking him up, then say "so long." He'd rather see Jemma and make sure she was okay.

He returned to the computer and checked up on Leslie. Her interest was gardening and not much else. No photos of her were loaded on the garden club website. Tucker checked on two of her children. The one with the priesthood was not active online. Her daughter was active on Twitter and some other social networking sites. She was into genealogy on her father's side and was still searching for information about her mother's family. She'd posted a photo of her mother from thirty years ago. An attractive woman despite the conservative dress and ugly shoes. Tucker printed the photo and taped it up beside the newer one on the conference room board before leaving work.

***

Friday early evening

Jemma was deep in thought as she seated herself at supper. So many suspects, so little time. She came out of her brain fog when Alma said, "Everyone's stupid until they're thirty, even women. They have children for the wrong reasons or too early. Kids get into taking chances."

"Weren't you young once?"

"Maybe. At this point, I've forgotten the experience. In my day, it was drugs, sex and rock and roll. Now it's extreme sports, texting while driving, tattoos and binge drinking."

"Is something wrong with having children?" Juanita asked.

"That's not what I meant. A woman should want to have children and spend the next twenty years raising them. She shouldn't have them because she can or by accident or because her parents want to be grandparents. Good grief. The planet is over crowded with people as it is. There are more poor people in India than there are humans in the whole of North America."

Randy said, "I know I was in my thirties before I started to figure out myself. I had to shift gears or I would have been six feet under before I was ripe. My dad told me to mend my broken bridges or else he'd disown me. I couldn't stand that."

"Disown? Is that like getting a divorce and being thrown out of the church?" Juanita asked.

Alma nodded. "Not all religions see divorce that way. Nowadays, some Catholics get divorced in this county."

"Leslie's Catholic," Jemma murmured.

"Who?" Bo asked. "I remember. The nice lady who took our pictures on Monday. Miguel thinks he saw her at church."

Alma stood and made the schedule announcement. "Riders, be ready at eight tomorrow morning for an all day ride with a breakfast cookout at Blue Falls. By now, your bodies should be in good enough condition to be in the saddle most of the day. Non-riders, you're leaving for historic downtown Boone at nine. In the evening, we'll have a gymkana competition to see if you riders have learned much this week about handling horses."

The phone rang and Jemma excused herself to answer it in the kitchen. The caller wanted to talk with Miguel so Jemma leaned through the doorway and motioned him over.

"Si, si. Gracious." Miguel said and hung up. To Jemma he said, "It's tonight at the same place. The cockfight."

"I'll call Tucker. Thanks Miguel."

"I must tell my friends."

"I understand. Can you call one and have him tell the others?" At his nod, she added, "They need to keep it to themselves. Don't let anyone else know to stay away. Understand?"

He nodded and called one person.

After he finished and returned to the dining room, Jemma called Tucker's cell phone number. "It's tonight," she said. "The cockfight's in about an hour at the same place as last time." Glasses tinkled in the background. "Are you at a bar?" Her heart thudded, rebelling against the thought of him with his old girlfriend.

"Jemma, don't jump to conclusions. I appreciate the notice. Promise you'll stay at the ranch. Let us take it from here."

"But I'm the one who knows the lay of the land." She stopped before admitting she worried about him. Gambling meant money. Money needed protection which meant guns.

"Give us some credit, will you? I want to be sure you're safe. Besides, we're going by the rules on this one. Too much is at stake."

"Wear your vest. Put the steel plate in the pocket over your heart. Be careful." Fear for Tucker overtook her need to be involved. She would only be a distraction.

"Yes, ma'am." His tone was neutral.

"Call me when it's over, no matter how late. Later, Gator." At least she knew he worried about her safety.

Her sanity was up to her. Jemma stopped by the ranch reception desk and chatted with her mother for a few minutes. She noticed a guest standing in front of one of her framed photographs.

Jemma walked over to her. "That's one of my favorite photographs of Blue Falls."

"It's beautiful. I love the way you captured the mist rising. The whole scene is so peaceful. Wish I had a copy to hang on my wall at home."

"I'll be happy to sell you one. Do you want me to frame it like this or would you prefer a darker wood?"

The woman turned and smiled. "I didn't realize I could actually take one home with me. That's wonderful. Use the same color wood, the same size print. Would you sign and date it for me?" The woman clapped her hands together softly, as if she were tickled pink.

"I'd be honored to sign it. It'll be ready by the time you check out on Sunday."

She told her mother about the sale and returned to her cabin where JK greeted her at the door. DT came in a few minutes later so she fed the kitties and locked them in for the night.

Jemma grabbed her hammer and crow bar and headed up stairs. The interior upstairs walls were not load bearing and were narrow wood slats, kind of like beadboard, so she pried away for a couple of hours, listening to the creak of the old nails pulling loose. In her mind, she ran a play by play of the gambling crack down.

In every scenario, Tucker remained in control and unscathed. She knocked out the nails from the old wood and piled it at the top of the stairs it to take down later. Each recovered board offered a sense of accomplishment, a substitute for squelching her CSI wannabe talents.

Chapter 18: Friday night

"I have to go," Tucker said to Wanda after ending the call from Jemma. "It was good to see you again."

"That's it? What about tomorrow?" Wanda hopped off the bar stool and followed Tucker to the door.

Tucker turned and took Wanda's hands into his. His thumb caressed the back of her hands. "I have to be honest. You were right. That's it. I'm too busy to make time every night for someone. Besides, what time I have, I'd rather spend with someone else. Thanks for looking me up." Tucker walked out the door and headed to his car.

"You can't do this to me," Wanda cried, scurrying in her high heels to catch up with him. "I've thought about you for years. And now, now that I'm here, you should want to be with me."

Tucker turned and looked her straight in the eyes. "I told you no. Besides, I'm not doing that again to your husband. He deserves better treatment from me and from you. Take care of yourself."

"Well, I never," she said in a huff, turned and retreated to the door, as if she expected him to change his mind.

Tucker opened the trunk, retrieved his vest and police belt. When he dropped the plate over his heart, Jemma's concern for him made him pause. Someone besides kin cared deeply for him. He put on a light jacket to cover his firepower.

Tucker pressed the button to unlock the door, punched his cell phone pad and spoke a few words to Graves while he got in and started the car. The image in his rear view mirror of Wanda standing alone in the brightly lit parking lot was somehow satisfying. He no longer felt the urge to wonder about Wanda.

The sun turned brilliant red against the many high clouds at the top of the mountain when Tucker turned onto Elk Creek Road, switching to radio since cell phone reception would be sparse from here. Half a mile down he turned on his lights when he drove into a cloud bank. His cousin had described it as so thick "you could wash your hands in the clouds." Although he knew the road well, he slowed for the three switchback curves and came out of the cloud after the third curve.

The road was dark, few houses had security lights in the valley. The sparsely populated area had more traffic than usual, all traveling in the same direction. The cars crossed Elk Creek just past the turn off to the road to Blue Falls Ranch and he hoped Jemma had listened to him and stayed home. He didn't want her trapped in the upcoming roundup.

He turned when the line of vehicles did and followed a creek up the narrow valley. From earlier reconnaissance, he knew the road opened up to a field on one side, many out buildings, an old farm house and a large barn. Forty or so vehicles were clustered in the field; a few belonged to undercover agents. He parked away from the rest of the crowd. When he sauntered into the nearby woods, he nodded to the half-dozen plain clothes officers waiting for the full force to arrive. Most he recognized even in the half-light; a few were new to the Boone police force.

Sharp voices rose from the direction of the road. Tucker soon realized it was two late coming hard-of-hearing guys trying to find their way to the fight in the twilight. They sounded like dueling talkers. "Forty thousand in prize money," one yelled. "I thought it was twenty-five dollars to watch," yelled the other.

Tucker's radio squawked. Tucker hoped he was far enough away from the action for the gamblers to notice. Graves' voice was soft. "We're set up on the right side of the road. Patrol is set at the entrance. Animal Control is parked on another side road along with transport buses."

"Make your way up to the arena on your side. Let me know when you are in position." Tucker motioned his people to follow him. Due to the layout of the property, they were in the open but the darkness helped conceal their movements. Tucker walked near the road at a deliberate pace to hide his excitement. The dense underbrush and rhododendron hells in the woods were too thick to use as cover. Over on the right side of the road was a hay field and the officers could walk along the far edge.

Tucker estimated the crowd at sixty, none of them Latino as far as he could see in the spotlighted arena. He fingered the warrant in his pocket. Cockfighting was now a felony in North Carolina. It was early enough that none of the roosters had fought yet. He'd seen the gruesome sharp metal gafts strapped to the rooster's legs before. These birds would not fight tonight.

Tucker went behind the barn, keyed his radio and spoke softly. "The ringleader is bringing in the gamecocks now. I'll go in and present the warrant. Half of your people need to be near the ring, the other half twenty feet behind them to catch those that make it through."

***

After an hour of demolition and with one wall removed, Jemma paced in her living room, aware that her two kitties watched in unnatural silence. "What?" she asked them. They only blinked. Then she heard it, a mouse squeak. The cats jumped to the floor and assumed the flat, patient, watching pose. JK seemed fully recovered from her afternoon ordeal. The mouse was a goner.

Jemma took the hint and sat at the computer with her own inanimate mouse. The Poison Control site was not much help. It mainly dealt with how to treat a poison victim and not an account of what to use. She went to Wikipedia and searched plants that grow in the North Carolina mountains. If an autopsy report could take months, no telling how long a toxicology report would take. Periodically, she looked at the clock wondering about the bust and if Tucker was safe. It was dark, he was near the woods. How many people were at the cockfight? Ugh. How pathetic for someone to even watch a fight, much less enjoy it. At least killing and eating an animal for food provided nourishment; this spectacle could only feed a lust for violence.

Scott had had convulsions. What besides arsenic caused that?

***

Tucker made his way through the crowd and approached the staging table just as the first two roosters were released to fight. The ringleader stepped back to let the gamblers have a place at the ring. Tucker handed the ringleader the warrant. "You're under arrest," he shouted to be heard over the crowd noise and grabbed the man's right arm, swung him around, grabbed the other and put handcuffs on him.

Sweat, dust and hay hung in the air. Most of the spectators were so absorbed in the fight, they didn't notice. If he could help it, no roosters would have eyes pierced, lungs punctured or bones broken tonight.

Graves and the other officers cuffed those furthest from the center and rounded them up behind the barn. All were white men of various ages from teen to cane-toting seniors. By the time a third of them had been secured, the others looked up from the fight and tried to escape, but it was too late. The escape road was blocked. A designated detective took photos of the round up.

Animal Control workers separated the two roosters. How they did it without being injured was beyond Tucker.

All in all, sixty-eight people were arrested. The judge was one of the first to get cuffed. He'd recognized the bust and tried to leave. "Don't know why I can't watch a cockfight. Our founding fathers, Washington and Jefferson, enjoyed it."

"They lived with slavery, too. Along with wives who couldn't vote." Tucker walked the judge to the round up area. "Judge, I'm surprised you'd come to a gathering like this. So much cash, tempers high. Some gun-carrying hothead could shoot you down, all because he lost a bet."

"That's not likely. Those birds like to fight."

"Only because they've been bred and trained like athletes. Shot up with steroids, too. In nature, they fight over females, food or territory and seldom get hurt. Plus, these birds are forced to fight regardless of how exhausted or hurt they are. Reminds me of the gladiators of old Rome."

"You may be right about that." The judge shrugged, straining against the cuffs. "You have to admit it's exciting."

"No. It's cruel. And against the law. If these birds were transported across state lines, the federal law kicks in. Jail time for that is three years."

The spectators were marched in groups of six to vans parked on the main road. An armed guard rode shotgun.

Fifty-three vehicles, twenty-four fire arms and fifty thousand in cash were seized along with cocaine and marijuana. Animal Control took possession of one hundred and twenty live roosters. Tucker had been right, none of the spectators had been Latino. He tapped the steel plate over his heart, thankful that no guns had been used that night.

***

Jemma's phone rang around four in the morning, waking her from a fitful sleep. "Did you get him?"

"The judge was picked up along with close to seventy others. I'm heading home to get a couple of hours sleep."

"Did anyone get hurt?" Jemma held her breath waiting for his answer.

"Only two of the fighting cocks. I, uh, appreciate the tip and that you stayed away. I have an idea of how hard that was for you."

Tucker was safe. "I had my own form of entertainment, getting a mouse away from two cats. I trapped it in a waste basket and released it up in the woods out back. JK and DT searched for that mouse for the rest of the night." Jemma sat up in bed. "I miss you, Gator," she whispered, afraid of his reaction.

"I miss you, C-girl. Get some sleep. I'll call when I get a chance."

"I'll tell you about what I found on local poisons. Good night."

Chapter 19: Saturday morning

The family refused to let Jemma lead the day long trail ride, fearing she might have a delayed reaction to the chili episode, so she forwarded to Tucker what she had found out about poisons, including jimsonweed, two types of hemlock, maybe horsechestnut—but it caused paralysis and not convulsions—foxglove, yew, mountain laurel and good old tobacco. Burley tobacco was still grown in the mountains but it wouldn't cause convulsions either. It was a wonder everyone up here didn't get poisoned.

He emailed back, inviting her to lunch at Mike's Inland Seafood. He'd been thinking about shrimp and missed her. Jemma's heart thumped when she read the last two words. She missed him, too.

After breakfast, she drove to Aaron's house. He was outside mowing the grass. He wanted to finish before it rained and told her to go inside and get some iced tea. Jemma thought about taking a relaxing time on the porch watching Aaron ride the mower back and forth.

Instead, she found herself in his bedroom, looking at his private photo collection. She recognized some of the women, she thought, as she flipped the pages of his album. She stopped on the fifth page at the photo of the judge's wife. Opposite it was one of Harold's wife. She flipped back through the pages and noted that in those photos with hands, all the women had wedding rings. The mower motor stopped and she started to put back the album but changed her mind. She stuck it under her arm, took it downstairs, grabbed tea for Aaron and walked out on the porch, feeling calmer than she ought.

"Why girl, what a snoop you are. Bold about it, too." Aaron nodded at the photo album, accepted the glass and sat on the porch swing where Jemma joined him.

She put the album on the side table. "Why married women?"

"Instead of men or instead of single women?"

"Both."

Aaron gulped down the sweet tea and put the glass on the porch railing. "My voice is sing-songy and a little high. People assumed I like men and after a while, I started using that as cover. I naturally appreciate the things some girly women like, fashion, gossip, shopping. You know as well as I do that women are comfortable around gay men because they don't hit on them."

Jemma looked down at her thrift shop outfit of fitted jeans, sandals and a brightly colored top, even she'd gone a bit "girly."

"You look good, by the way. Much better than the men's clothes you used to wear. I meet lots of women while cleaning teeth. Shortly after I moved here, one of the married ones hit on me. I was surprised since my gay cover had become second nature. She was lonely. We were discrete but she and her husband moved off the mountain a few months later. Attracting married women was easier than finding a single one. The single ones have a long list of what a man should be like and I'm not like that. I don't fix things, I seldom get angry, and I have a woman's job."

"Did you ever get caught?"

He shook his head and smiled. "The husbands are surprisingly clueless. Plus, the wives know when to call it quits. It's all fun for me so I don't argue but thank them for a wonderful affair."

"Do they give you gifts?"

"Some of them. Usually photography equipment since I don't wear diamonds, darling. Mostly we have quiet evenings here. Some only want to talk. Others only want sex. I'm available for both or either."

Jemma listened to the squeak of the chain as they swung. "Sounds lonely to me."

"I have to admit, it's getting old. But you're already taken so what can I do?" Aaron nudged her arm.

Jemma laughed. "I'll take that as a compliment. Tucker has some single women cousins you might be interested in. What do you think?"

"Would you settle for a 'maybe'?"

"Whatever you want." They swung in silence for a moment. "What do you think of Tammy?"

"I wouldn't mind getting to know her better. She's single, so you'd approve. She's attractive, mature and strong, all qualities I admire."

"Does she remind you of your momma?"

Aaron stopped the swing. "Oh, girl, I never thought of that." He sipped some tea. "Don't get me wrong, I love my momma but I don't need someone to take care of me. I like to do the fussin' over someone."

"Tammy could use someone who cares for her." Especially if she goes to jail. Tucker never did tell what he'd found out about the horse doping last year.

"She worked so hard on Scott. I couldn't stop watching until you shooed us out of there. She was magnificent." Aaron's eyes shown with excitement at the memory.

"Did Scott know about this?" Jemma picked up the photo album from the side table.

"Not that he ever mentioned. He'd been to the house a time or two for parties. You found my hiding place; he could have."

"What would you have done if he'd confronted you?"

"Ask him to be discrete. Those women are fine people and I'd hate to see harm come to them because of me. I'd lie to protect them."

"Would you do more than that?"

"Maybe. Depends. But I didn't kill him, and I don't believe Tammy had anything to do with it either."

"What about the ipecac in the chili? Did one of your lady friends get miffed?"

Aaron glanced at the album. "Maybe. "

Jemma handed Aaron the album and stood. "Thanks for the tea. Let me know what you decide about Tucker's cousins."

Jemma's cell phone rang after she turned out of Aaron's driveway. Jemma told Tucker about the affair with both Harold's and the judge's wives but asked Tucker to try to leave Aaron out of it.

"Like you kept Miguel and his friends out of the round up last night?"

Jemma gulped. "You figured it out."

***

"It doesn't make sense," Tucker said to Graves while they prepared to interview the judge in the interrogation room. "If jealousy were the motive, why kill Scott? Why not kill Aaron?"

After talking with the deflated judge about his role in the cockfight tournament, Tucker said, "Just supposing, you found out your wife was having an affair. What would you do?"

The judge's chest swelled with indignation. "She wouldn't dare. She's married to me. She holds an important position in this community and wouldn't jeopardize that." He looked down at his hands and shook his head, apparently realizing that he'd done just that.

"But what if she did." Tucker figured the judge would gain status in some parts of the county over the cock fighting.

The judge squinted. "I'd ruin him. Don't know how but I'd run him out of town. Then I'd put a chastity belt on my wife." His eyes widened. "Say, did Scott have an affair with Harold's wife?" He mentioned a few other married men in the photography club. "Are you testing out a hypothesis on me?"

"How did you guess?"

The judge quieted. "My career's ruined by this. I know I should have stayed away but the fight was so thrilling. I felt alive when I watched it. I'm going to miss that more than anything else. We both know I'll get off with a fine and a misdemeanor since I was just a spectator. My wife's been wanting to move to Florida and get away from the winters up here. It might be time to retire and do that."

"What about the gambling part?"

The judge looked sideways at Tucker and relaxed his shoulders. "Why Tucker, I do believe you want to add 'gambling' to the charges against me."

Tucker flashed a smile. "Covering all the bases, Judge. We think Scott knew about the cockfights. Did you see him there?"

"No." He shook his head. "This is only the second one I've ever been to. I went to one years ago, and it has been on my mind ever since then. When I overheard about the tournament from one of the Mexicans, I gave into my temptation. God is my witness."

"We have a statement from someone who saw you on Tuesday night at the same place."

"Oh, well, I forgot about that. I've been the three fights. That's all. I swear."

Tucker escorted the judge to the front door; he'd been released earlier that morning. The judge had spent a few hours in the old part of the cinder block jail with an eight by ten cell equipped with a toilet and cot.

Tucker wondered if he'd be haunted by others who had spent time in those cells.

Tammy had spent the night in the female section without individual cells as the women were all housed in the same room. Toilets and showers were in the open area. The privilege of privacy was non-existent.

***

Tucker arrived a few minutes early for his lunch date with Jemma. He selected a table by the window and sat facing the entry. He ordered sweet tea for himself and water for Jemma. So much had happened, a decade seemed to have passed since he saw her before the murder on Monday.

Jemma entered and looked around for him. Her tentative smile echoed his own feelings at the moment. Tucker stood and took in every detail of her, shiny shoulder length hair, long narrow jeans, colorful blouse. She belonged on the cover of a magazine. As she approached, his body flooded with excitement. Whatever he had done in the past week with Wanda couldn't be allowed to damage his relationship with Jemma, his C-girl.

"Hi. Have you been waiting long?" Jemma asked, sitting in the cane bottom chair he'd pulled out for her.

"Forever," he whispered, caught himself, then shook his head and sat awkwardly while the server left a basket of hushpuppies. "I'll have the Calabash shrimp, fried. Do you know what you want, Jemma?"

"Same thing, only broiled." After the server left, Jemma immediately asked about the investigation.

Tucker groaned. "You know I can't tell you about an on-going investigation."

"Fair enough. Did you know that Aaron's going public about being straight? Tammy impressed him so much he's going to ask her out. Do you know if she competed in the riding tournament yesterday?"

Tucker thought carefully before speaking. "She decided to back off and ride for pleasure. Like a lot of people, she fell into the trap of wanting revenge. Winning the trophy with her ex's family name on it was her focus for many years."

"Bless her heart, as Alma would say. She'd also say that people have the right to make bad choices. Tammy did go on and on about the horse show."

"Her judgment failed her. The trophy in her house would have been a constant reminder of a family she'd rather forget. Maybe Aaron would be a welcomed distraction." He hadn't actually disclosed any confidential information. Jemma should be satisfied with his implication that Tammy wasn't the killer.

"Who knows? She could introduce him to riding

and they could go off into the sunset together." Jemma sipped her water, then tapped her fingers on the glass. "I'll bet the judge regrets his lack of judgment. Cockfighting is so repulsive. He had a huge secret to protect."

"That's true." Tucker hoped she wouldn't pry for more details.

Jemma took the hint and asked about having to tell Scott's parents about the death and chatted about the ranch. Her words tumbled on top of each other. Some things were repeats of their phone discussions. She toyed with a spoon on the table.

None of her talk was personal, almost as if she were afraid to bring up the subject of Wanda. How would Tucker handle life if her ex-boyfriend showed up and she went out with him? He'd be direct and ask her what her intentions were. He had hurt his C-girl without much forethought.

Tucker reached over and covered her hand with his. He squeezed gently and said, "I owe you an explanation."

Jemma shook her head. She tried to remove her hand, but Tucker held tight. She switched to a nod. "Yes, you do."

Tucker released her hand and they both leaned back in their chairs. Tucker took a calming breath. "I've never been comfortable talking about myself. I always figured it was my boring past and no one was really interested."

"I'm interested." Jemma didn't smile.

"Wanda was an affair that hit me when I was in my early twenties. It started, then I found out she was married, and I didn't end it. I'm not proud of that. At that time, I didn't care. All I wanted was her." He glanced away. The pressure of confession intensified and he blinked a couple of times.

Jemma sat quietly.

Tucker looked back to Jemma, determined to finish. "Her husband changed jobs and they moved away. I never had another serious relationship until you. That's what's important to me now." Whew, his under arms were wet and he slowly wiped his hands on his pant legs. The hard part was over. He'd confessed to Jemma.

Jemma smiled at the server when she placed their plates in front of them and refilled their drinks. "Is that it? Are you finished? You didn't tell me a thing about what happened this week."

Tucker grabbed a hushpuppy and stuffed it into his mouth, thinking while he chewed. Jemma stared at him. "I kissed her a couple of times and realized that I wanted to be with you. She doesn't mean anything to me anymore, and even the memory of the old romance died. When I found out she was still married, I walked away. To you, if you'll have me." Tucker gulped down sweet tea, again relieved that ordeal was over.

"She's still married. Did you think of me before or after you found that out?" Her inflection was neutral, neither accusing or excusing. Jemma speared some of the shrimp with a fork and lifted them to her mouth.

Tucker watched her movement carefully before realizing that she had on make-up. It was subtle and pretty, but it was another change that went along with her hair cut. He leaned forward and put both hands on the table. "Both, all the time, even when I worked on the case. C-girl, you are on my mind constantly, which can be a problem." Especially when the other detectives reminded him of the clues she'd found. She took this much better than Graves had prepared him for.

Move on to another topic. "I, uh, also appreciate you

passing along information about Scott's murder as you find it. In the past, you took it upon yourself to follow up on your own. This is a big improvement. Especially since you got sick and all. And it has helped me keep my job." His strong, solid and deserved compliment should work.

"Aunt Alma agreed with your boss so I'm behaving. Besides, I'm busy at the ranch. Which reminds me, I must go and do some errands for Alma. Thank you for the lunch." Jemma tapped her mouth with her napkin and stood to leave.

Tucker grabbed the napkin from his lap and rose from his chair. "So soon? You didn't eat much. I still have a few minutes and had hoped we could visit for a while."

"We'll talk later."

Tucker plopped down in his chair. What was that all about? He watched Jemma's long, strong back as she walked away. He finished his lunch and the leftover shrimp on her plate before realizing that Jemma was up to something.

Chapter 20: Saturday Afternoon

Jemma almost stumbled out of the restaurant, afraid she'd run back in and yell at Tucker. Instead, she followed Juanita's advice and kept it cool, agreeable and short. Leave him wondering and wanting. At least she knew Tammy was no longer a suspect. Besides, she did have an errand to run.

She drove to Leslie's home and found her working in the lower garden. "Alma wanted me to pick up that mint you offered. She's found a place to put a planter near the front porch."

"After we dig up the mint, let's go in and have some mint tea. How's your stomach doing? It'll help settle it. My appetite's not yet back to normal."

They walked up the hillside path between terraced gardens open to the sun. "Our house was built on a former cow pasture so the trees were cut decades before." Leslie pointed to the rock walls. "We had to clear the garden plots and had plenty of rocks for the walls and paths."

They quickly walked up one terraced section. "I recognize those. Coneflowers, aren't they?" The tomato plants looked good. One terrace had corn stalks with beans growing alongside.

"Correct. On the far end near the woods are Joe-pye weeds. They'll be a bright red in the fall."

Jemma paused, hearing Leslie's exhales. "May we cut over to the trail next to the woods?" The last thing Jemma wanted to do was cause Leslie a heart attack. She shouldn't be working in the hot sun on a steep hillside.

"Sure, we own that land, too."

Jemma asked about a large shrub growing on level ground Leslie answered that it was called a Black Willow, then walked in the shade up a more meandering path. Azaleas had already bloomed, the royal ferns were lush in the dappled light, and jewelweed stood tall though it wouldn't have blossoms until late summer. Jemma noted mayapple deeper in the woods, before they walked back into the sun and across the top terraced garden.

Leslie used a trowel to dig up the mint and drop it into a plastic container. Jemma offered to pay for the plant but Leslie refused. "I don't know how much longer I'll be able to keep up this garden. My husband wants me to work only this top terrace. My knees hurt more after a weeding session."

"This hillside is steep. You could plant some wild flowers and let them take over."

"True enough. We give away most of the vegetables now that the children are grown."

"Do you mind having a cow pasture next door?" Jemma asked, walking on level ground to the far end of the garden.

"Not really. Their lowing can be calming. They do muddy up the stream sometimes. Most of the time, they're on the other side of the land, near the barn and farmhouse."

"What's that pretty flower?" Jemma pointed to a purple-mottled stem with small white clustered blossoms.

"Water hemlock, some call it cowbane. The farmer is usually good about destroying it. I'll have to call him and let him know he has missed a crop."

Jemma followed Leslie to a shed where she put away the trowel. Hanging from the rafters were all kinds of dried herbs and plants. "I sell some at the Saturday Farmer's Market," Leslie said when she saw Jemma staring at the bundles.

In the kitchen, she saw a mortar and pestle for grinding seeds and such. Leslie explained that she combined components in a baggie to use as teas or to add to sour cream or yogurt for dips. The walls and table tops were festooned with photos of flowers, kids and her husband. A large Catholic cross dominated a corner along with a framed Indulgence.

"Go ahead and wash up in the sink. Have you heard anything about Scott's murderer?" Leslie asked.

"Not yet. It's a shame. Scott wouldn't hurt anyone. I can't imagine why someone would want to kill him."

"He was a reporter. Wasn't it his job to investigate and expose things?"

"He wasn't out for sensational type reporting, if that's what you mean." Jemma washed her hands. "Why, Leslie, do you have something to hide?" She teased with an underlay of genuine interest.

"Me? You flatter me. No. Not in the least." Leslie handed Jemma a paper towel to dry her hands. "I confess my little sins to the priest every month. All I have is gratitude for the life I'm living. My children are grown and contributing to society. My husband and I are both healthy. Our mortgage is paid off. I have my garden. No snakes in this garden of Eden."

***

Tucker headed out Hwy 194 toward Todd to follow up on the lady being harassed by Harold and the others. He turned off 194, crossed the river, turned back onto a gravel road and finally approached a lone old log cabin near the river. Moss grew on the roof shingles; a tall weed grew up from the gutter. From the looks of things, Harold's property backed up to this one. It was secluded, all right. The nearest neighbor was across the river and up a piece. No one around for a solo woman to call for help. No wonder the lady was spooked.

Two pickup trucks held household goods and two men loaded a dresser into the back of one of them. They pointed inside when Tucker showed his badge. The lady inside had her hands on her hips and seemed to be taking a last look around.

"Gave up on us?" Tucker asked after showing his badge.

She nodded. "A friend from work told me about a rental near town and I immediately canceled my lease on this place. The owner, a woman who lives in Florida, understood and even agreed to give me back my deposit."

"Mind if I look around?"

"Have at it. Lock the door behind you. I'm out of here. All that's left for me to do is mail the landlady the key and change my electricity account. FYI, someone stood on my porch last night while I was packing. I turned off the light and hid to the side of the window until he left. It was too dark to tell much about him."

"You sure it was a 'him'?"

"Tall, skinny and loopy trot to get away from here."

Tucker figured she didn't want to be further involved but appreciated her sketch of the man. Must have been one of the other two she'd reported. After she left, Tucker went over the small cabin but didn't find any signs of a secret storage area for drugs or stolen jewels. None of the loose floorboards yielded when he pried under them with a knife. There were no closets or an attic. The few kitchen cabinets were empty. The low crawl space under the house held undisturbed cobwebs.

A walk around the outside of the house revealed multiple shoe prints in the damp ground. Tucker headed to the rock in the river, a couple hundred feet in front of the cabin. A squirrel chatted at him; a blue jay squealed. The river rushed by the rock and formed a whirlpool below before hitting rapids. Great for canoes in high water like now; too much for tubing even in dry times. Trout could lurk near the edge of the river, especially when they stocked the waters.

Tucker could make out a roof up the hill, half a mile above the cabin. He headed in that direction, following a deer trail. The hostas by the house had been chewed down as had the lower branches on the rhododendron. The woods calmed him, as usual, even though he sought clues to human activity. Patches of the low broad leafed mayapple dotted the woods. Their single bloom had passed, replaced by a tiny apple that would mature in the fall. What part of that plant was poisonous?

Why would those guys run off a young woman like that? Had the cabin been used for poker? It was too remote for drug dealers. No trash dump or other evidence of a meth lab. The renter would have had to clean all that up, and he doubted she would have leased the place if she had seen anything like that.

Tucker struck off the trail when he saw boulders, careful to watch for snakes. Black snakes were fine and useful for keeping the bug population down. Elevation was too high for copperheads, unlike down in Triplett and at Jemma's ranch. Using a stick, he poked into crevices, overturned branches and moved small rocks. Deep in one crevice, he saw a neon pink color and used his flashlight to look closer. He snapped a photo, carefully scraped out the remains of a gelatin casing, and put it into a plastic baggie. Harold had held true to form.

Tucker made his way through the woods and up the hill to the house he'd seen the roof of when he was standing on the rock in the river. Now that he knew what he was looking for, he caught sight of a few more neon splotches under branches and protected dry spots along the trail.

"Detective?" Harold met him at the edge of the trees in his back yard. "Never expected you to show up on this side of my house."

Tucker stopped a few feet short of Harold and matched his wide-legged stance. "Following up on that complaint from your neighbor. The trail is easy to follow if you know what you're looking for."

"Not too many people would see the signs."

"Hard to fool a local boy. Trackin' and huntin's in our blood."

Harold turned and walked to a wood bench beside his deck. "Care for a beer?"

"Another time. I'm working." Tucker followed him and sat at the other end of the bench. He sat quietly and took in the deep green trees, the Carolina blue sky and the flutter of goldfinches around a bird feeder. "There's a good crop of mayapples down the hill."

Harold looked sideways at Tucker. "Oh, yeah? What do they look like?"

"Not into plants?" Tucker guessed as much.

"I like trees and such, but the little ones escape me. Ask me about animals and their habits. Those I can talk about."

"I solved one mystery today."

"You know who killed Scott?"

"Maybe." Tucker pulled from his pocket the baggie with the neon gel casing and handed it to Harold.

Harold didn't touch it but frowned.

"Want to tell me about it?"

"It has nothing to do with Scott. And nothing personal with the girl. We was just protecting our rights." Harold gulped from his beer can.

"What rights would that be?"

"Before the cabin owner died last year, we was allowed to hunt on his land. We'd stopped that years ago but then a group of us turned to paint ball skirmishes. A dozen of us meet once a month and play war." Harold stood and stretched his back. "The cabin was off limits. We never used it for hiding but knew the perimeter was fifty feet around the building. We was careful to avoid shooting the cabin."

"Why run off the woman? The landlady would have told her about the one day a month she needed to be careful." Tucker remained seated, watching Harold as he paced.

"Like I said, he died. She didn't exactly give us permission to use the land when we politely asked. Since she never came here and lived in Florida, we continued like before. All was fine until that rental lady moved in."

"You figured you'd get her to move out and you could return to your games, right?"

"Something like that." Harold finished his beer and

looked directly at Tucker.

"You ignored the 'No Trespassing' signs I passed on the walk here. New ones, from the look of them."

"Arrest me, then, for trespassing. I had nothing to do with Scott's death."

Tucker waited for Harold to return to his seat. He tucked the evidence baggie back into his pocket. "The landlady hasn't made a formal complaint so I'll keep this for reference."

"We'll figure out somewhere else to play our games. One of the fellas may know someone who'll give us permission."

Tucker had kept the peace and was about to leave when Harold sat up a little straighter.

"I just remembered something, but it may not be important. The judge rented Leslie a house when she first came here twenty-five years ago. She was quiet even then. Didn't like to talk about herself. He helped her get a driver's license. She'd lost hers when her house burned down near Charlotte. The judge said that Leslie married within a year, moved in with her husband and had her first child a year after that. She and the judge's wife both belong to the garden club so the judge had kept up with her. Then they re-met at the photography club."

Tucker thanked Harold and walked down through the woods back to his car. Tucker returned to work, hit the computer and searched for old missing person cases. After a frustrating few hours, he found a photo that matched the one on Leslie's daughter's Facebook page. Tucker called the detective listed on the cold case files for details. The missing person's name was Karen Douglas Voght. Her husband was remarried and still alive. Tucker called the husband.

Chapter 21: Saturday Afternoon

She shouldn't have left him at lunch like that, Jemma told herself as she drove to the Watauga County Law Enforcement Center. What worked for Juanita didn't sit right with her.

Jemma glanced in the rear view mirror then tilted her face so she could see her reflection. The hair cut was right; the clothes felt good but the game with Tucker left her feeling worse. Now was the time to correct that. She'd wait by his desk until he could see her. Besides, he needed to know that Leslie worked with herbs and had knowledge about local plants. She had an excuse to be there.

"He'll be back soon," Graves said when he pulled up a chair next to Tucker's desk. "Keep it short. We've planned a video conference call and he doesn't have time for socializing."

Jemma started to ask but Graves stopped her with a shake of his head. It had to be about Scott's death; that case would be a priority over all the others. A jumble of objects on Tucker's desk caught her eye. Shot glass and rooster. Wait a minute, Jemma thought, the shot glass could be for Scott and the rooster for the judge. The woman athletic doll had to be for Summer, and the man doll in a tuxedo must be for Aaron. "Graves, are these about the case?"

Graves looked over from his computer and nodded.

The gun stood for Harold, the flower for Leslie and the horse must be for Tammy. Jemma picked up the alligator and studied it closely. Kind of handsome in its own right. That left the cat.

"Figured it out yet?" Tucker asked from behind her.

Jemma dropped the figure as if guilt dripped from her hand. "You scared me."

He squeezed her shoulder, then rounded her and sat in his chair. "I'm glad to see you, but …"

Jemma held up a palm to interrupt. "I know. You have something important to do. I wanted to apologize for leaving so abruptly after lunch. That was rude."

Tucker leaned forward. "It caught my attention. Mind if I come down tonight? I hope to wrap things up here in a few hours."

His face was only inches from hers. Jemma licked her lip to keep from closing the gap between them. "May I stay here? I'll be quiet." She would beg if she had to. He had the answers, he'd found the killer.

Tucker rolled back in his chair and looked at her.

"I'll sit in the lobby. I'll hide in the bathroom."

"You'll be bored, waiting for me."

"For what it's worth, I visited Leslie this afternoon." Jemma picked up the plastic flower from the pile on Tucker's desk. "She has all kinds of plants, herbs, dried things at her place. Gardening is her passion. Scott must have found out something about her."

"Much as I hate to deny you, you have to leave." Tucker stood.

"I know. It's none of my business." Jemma agreed to go but asked one more question. "Am I right? Is it Leslie?"

Tucker gathered up some papers from his desk, took her elbow and escorted her out. "I'll tell you tonight."

Tucker watched her leave the building, feeling as if something had settled between them. Maybe it was only on his part, he thought when he entered the conference room and set up the Skype equipment, but his secret past had been aired and now it was done with.

Graves escorted Leslie into the conference room a few minutes later.

"We have someone who wants to speak with you," Graves said, pulling out a chair for Leslie to sit in. He pushed the record button on a video camera set up at an angle to include both the monitor and Leslie.

"That's nice." Her voice shook a little.

Tucker pushed a button on the Skype and a man's face lit up the monitor. Tucker stayed off camera and watched Leslie's face change from anticipation, to puzzlement, to horror.

"No," she whispered.

"Hello, Karen. I couldn't be sure that was you from the photos. You've changed some but your eyes look the same." The man's voice remained calm and even. He'd been briefed and had had a little time to adjust to the news.

Leslie's eyes watered and her mouth quivered.

Tucker didn't want to waste time with a crying jag. "Years ago, the police spent a lot of time and taxpayer's money dragging that river looking for your body. Did this man harm you? You could have pressed charges."

Leslie looked at Tucker, then back at the monitor.

"No. He was very good to me. We loved each other."

The husband frowned. "Why did you leave me? For years, when your body wasn't found, I kept hoping you'd turn up."

Leslie put her hands over her heart. "You were sterile. We couldn't have children. I'm Catholic and couldn't get a divorce. I wanted children so badly."

"We could have done something. There are medical procedures."

"Not back then, or at least, I didn't know about them. Please understand, you were wonderful to me. I kept praying for an answer and 'run away' was the answer that came to me."

"That's it? What a terrible thing to do to me. You didn't love me, not real love. Detective, can we finish this? I've identified her and never want to see her again. My current wife is long-suffering. Finally we can put this, this mistake in my early life to rest."

Tucker moved to be on camera. "If you'll fax us a written statement, we'll be done. The detective will send a hard copy later. We appreciate your cooperation." Tucker clicked the "off" button after he'd heard a heartfelt "thank you" from the husband.

He turned and faced the sweet-looking killer. "You have the right to a lawyer."

"What good will that do me? I have sinned in the eyes of God. No torture you do to me will lessen the fate I have in store for me. Ask anything you want." Her eyes were dry and slightly vacant.

"What poison did you use?"

Leslie smiled a little smile. "It was right at Jemma's feet this afternoon. Cowbane, officially known as cicuta maculata, water hemlock. It grows in wet meadows and pastures. A walnut-sized portion of the root will kill a cow so I used less than that."

"How did you fix it?"

"I dried it and ground it into a powder with my pestle and mortar. It was supposed to act on him within thirty minutes. It took less time than that so I probably used too much. I simply dropped it into his drink. He wouldn't have been able to taste it, but I was worried about how it would react with the acid in the tomato juice."

"That was not a problem."

"No. He died as expected."

***

Tucker knocked on Jemma's cabin door, glad that she'd taken his advice and locked it. When she opened the door, he reached for her and held her tight. "Missed you," he murmured into her hair.

She pulled him into the living room and kissed him until he had to come up for air. Later, he answered most of her questions. Twenty, thirty years ago, getting a driver's license and new identity was easy. Leslie had gone to a cemetery and used the name of a child that had been born in the year she'd been born and had died before age eighteen. She applied for a Social Security number and began a new life. She married the first man who was kind to her and of her faith.

"Why kill Scott? Why now?"

He held her hand, needing to touch Jemma as he talked. "He'd taken a photograph of her at the library computer. She'd been researching the details of the search to find her body. It had made headlines. Leslie couldn't afford to have her past exposed. Not only would it hurt her children and her husband, but she'd be excommunicated from the church. I'm not sure that's true, but she believed the church would turn its back on her. More importantly, the stain would affect her son's career in the priesthood."

"Leaving a good man, killing another one—all for biological children? Somewhere along the line, her priorities got mixed up. She could have adopted." Jemma squeezed his hand. "What about the laptop?"

"She took it thinking that deleting the photo would keep her safe. Did I thank you for your help in this case? I appreciate that you tried to stay out of it." He leaned in close.

"I did a good job of that, didn't I? Would you care to show me some of that appreciation? Sometimes words aren't enough."

Jemma was so right.

THE END

Meet the atthor:

Maggie Bishop

Maggie's enjoyment of CSI TV, her love for the Appalachian Mountains and outdoor activities collectively have shaped her mystery series. Maggie has hiked, skied, climbed mountains and vacationed on several guest ranches around the country. She created the dude ranch where Jemma Chase lives outside of Boone, North Carolina, because she "thought we needed one."

Residents of Boone will recognize several local "characters" among the regulars at the ranch and in town. Some may even believe they recognize friends or even themselves among victims and suspects, but they are, of course, mistaken, as all the central characters are completely fictitious.

Maggie settled in the Appalachian Mountains in 1993 with her husband and cat. She founded High Country Writers in 1995 and the organization has grown from a dozen at the start to over 70 members in 2010. ***One Shot Too Many*** is her fifth novel set in the area. Her work has gained popularity and has been featured in regional and national publications such as the Houston Chapter of Sisters in Crime publication as a recommended mystery author, Midwest Book Review and Our State Magazine. She was selected ln 2007 as one of "100 Incredible Women" from East Carolina University.

Learn more about author Maggie Bishop
on her websites:
http://maggiebishop1.tripod.com
www.damesofdialogue.wordpress.com

Perfect for Framing
by Maggie Bishop

trade paperback —$12
ISBN: 9781932158847

GREED, jealousy and lust for power are a deadly mix when individual freedoms clash with group desires in this mountain subdivision. Returning for a second suspense-filled mystery, Jemma Chase and Detective Tucker find themselves embroiled in a Propery-Owners Association power struggle. When a simple break-in escalates to murder, Tucker finds suspects aplenty in POA president Petula Winsor's files, leading him to suspect the victim of blackmail. Tucker tries his best to keep Jemma's interest at bay. But when the POA president's husband is also found dead, and Tucker's life is in jeopardy, Jemma won't be stopped until she finds the guilty party.

Once more, Maggie Bishop delivers a thrilling whodunit, peppered with lovable characters and set against the beautiful backdrop of the mountains of North Carolina. Packed with breath-taking action and nail-biting suspense, with a twisting plot that guarantees constant speculation, this is one book that will have readers quickly turning pages, eager to find out what happens next. Highly recommended.
—Christy Tillery French, *Midwest Book Review*

Murder at Blue Falls
by Maggie Bishop

$12 —trade paperback
ISBN: 9781932158755

The horse found the body...

JEMMA Chase believes she just wants peace and believes she'll find it leading trail rides and doing carpentry on her parent's dude ranch in the Triplett Valley. A series of minor crimes escalates to arson and murder. Jemma's diversion as an amateur CSI provides her with procedures to do her own investigation but ultimately puts her life in danger. Detective Tucker's suspicions disturb and annoy our heroine, but when Jemma is kidnapped, Tucker is literally a lifesaver.

What a treat to read! ... finish the sequel soon.
—Deborah Hooper, WFMY News 2, Greensboro, NC

**Learn more about author Maggie Bishop
on her websites:
http://maggiebishop1.tripod.com
www.damesofdialogue.wordpress.com**

Appalachian Adventure Romance

Emeralds in the Snow
by Maggie Bishop
trade paperback - $12
ISBN: 9781932158564

EMERALD Graham and Lucky Tucker are an unlikely pair. She, accustomed to a life of privilege in which everything's a bit of a game, including her teaching career. He, who has not let his life of struggle keep him from giving to his family, his community and the skiers he rescues on Sugar Mountain. Yet they seem to be finding an uneasy bliss when a treasure hunt and an old murder mystery threaten all they value.

Appalachian Paradise
by Maggie Bishop
$9.95, trade paperback
ISBN:9780971304567

SUZANNE'S plan to hike alone to "get the city grime off her body" is thwarted by her uncle and father who con Wes into being a reluctant escort. Appalachian born Wes triggers Suzanne's resentment and her desire in a mountain hike amongst boars, bears and Girl Scouts. Suzanne's pack and old hurts lighten as Wes' charms help her see the allure of spring flowers forgiveness and love..

For more about
fine works of fiction and memoir from
Ingalls Publishing Group, Inc.
visit the website:
www.ingallspublishinggroup.com

Learn more about
author Maggie Bishop
on her websites:
http://maggiebishop1.tripod.com
www.damesofdialogue.wordpress.com

CPSIA information can be obtained at www.ICGtesting.com
Printed in the USA
238265LV00001B/7/P